Ecstasy Romance®

**"Your heroine did wonderful things with her
tongue in *Passion's Pawn*,"**

Eric whispered, opening the rest of his buttons
more quickly himself.

"I'm not my heroine!" Brenda backed away so
abruptly she nearly fell, feeling red heat rush to
her face.

"What's wrong?" He stood and followed her,
looking genuinely puzzled.

"I write fantasy! I'm not one of my heroines;
I'm in no way like them!"

"I haven't insulted you! I liked Gina in your
book. She's lively and fun and sexy in a positive
way."

"But she isn't me! Just please leave, Eric."

"I wasn't forcing myself on you. Just tell me
why the sudden turnoff."

"I didn't want this trip, and I don't want to
make love."

"You did a few minutes ago."

"That was a terrible mistake."

"You're making the terrible mistake," he said,
exasperated. "I think that you're fighting yourself,
not me."

A CANDLELIGHT ECSTASY ROMANCE®

HAPPILY EVER AFTER

Barbara Andrews

A CANDLELIGHT ECSTASY ROMANCE®

Published by
Dell Publishing Co., Inc.
1 Dag Hammarskjold Plaza
New York, New York 10017

To Mark

Dell ® TM 681510, Dell Publishing Co., Inc.

Candlelight Ecstasy Romance®, 1,203,540, is a registered
trademark of Dell Publishing Co., Inc., New York,
New York.

ISBN: 0-440-13439-0

Printed in the United States of America

First printing—October 1984

To Our Readers:

We have been delighted with your enthusiastic response to Candlelight Ecstasy Romances®, and we thank you for the interest you have shown in this exciting series.

In the upcoming months we will continue to present the distinctive, sensuous love stories you have come to expect only from Ecstasy. We look forward to bringing you many more books from your favorite authors and also the very finest work from new authors of contemporary romantic fiction

As always, we are striving to present the unique, absorbing love stories that you enjoy most—books that are more than ordinary romance.

Your suggestions and comments are always welcome. Please write to us at the address below.

Sincerely,

The Editors
Candlelight Romances
1 Dag Hammarskjold Plaza
New York, New York 10017

CHAPTER ONE

"Make way, ladies, make way. We gotta get this tank through. Make way there."

Brenda tried to shrink herself to get out of the way, nearly sitting on the edge of one of the tables lining the foyer to the ballroom, annoyed by the patronizing male voice and berating herself because she never stood up to the boors of the world. Just because this greasy-looking man was half a foot taller than anyone else in the congested area didn't mean he should shove his tank of helium through the crowd like a paramedic scattering a flock of chickens. Why did she let herself be intimidated by a person who filled balloons for a living and talked as if he had a clothespin pinching his nose?

Inching her way through the predominantly female crowd of writers, readers, and booksellers, she spotted a poster of her latest release, *Passion's Pawn,* propped on an easel behind the table manned by her publishing company. Even though her advance copies had arrived before she left for the Romance Conference, she was stunned by the impact of the cover, not quite believing she'd written the book herself. Seeing a blown-up version of her golden-haired heroine about to be kissed by

9

a bare-chested man with the face and build of a legendary god made the whole scene unreal. What was a quiet kid from Charlotte, Illinois, doing at the Roosevelt Hotel in New York playing the part of an award-winning author?

She'd never forgive Julie for backing out of the trip at the last minute, leaving her to face hordes of strangers on her own. What was a sister for if she stayed home just because a barn burned down? Brenda grinned inwardly, knowing how unfair she was being. Even dangling on the edge of panic, she could sympathize with her brother-in-law's problems. A farmer who lost half of his equipment in the spring needed his wife more than she did; unscrambling the insurance mess and trying to replace everything would be a full-time job for Julie for months.

The crowd packed between the two rows of tables began to thin out as people moved into the ballroom where a continental breakfast was being served as part of the opening morning program. Brenda's mouth was so dry her tongue felt glued to the roof, but she was sure that even a swallow of water would run down her chin. Nothing could get past her constricted throat muscles. Her pink badge, with its sparkling red heart designating her as a published author, was all she needed to pass through a doorway into a large area where buoyant balloons bobbed toward the ceiling. She hoped the obnoxious man with the helium wasn't getting rich on the conference, but the balloons did add to the festive feeling reflected on faces all around her.

Through another entryway she could see the ballroom itself, packed now with round cloth-covered tables. Pink flowers and balloons gave the spacious room a more romantic atmosphere, but Brenda couldn't enjoy any of it knowing she'd soon be the center of attention. If she went home now, would they mail her award? It was tempting, but how could she explain to her editor, her agent, her parents, her sister, her friends, and half the town of Charlotte that she'd been too scared to walk the long length of the ballroom and receive the coveted Sheffield Bookshelf Award for best-selling contemporary romance author of the year? Even if she fainted on someone's prune Danish, she had to make the trek between the tables when they called her name.

Nearly tripping on a thick black cable called her attention to a network cameraman, only one of many members of the press sent to cover the opening of the conference. With her luck—bad luck—she might make national television. A knot larger than her stomach made her feel like doubling over, and she was sure her gizzard would have permanent kinks. Even if she remembered her very short acceptance speech, two sentences to be delivered with terrified sincerity, the words probably couldn't escape from her throat.

Everyone around her seemed to be having a marvelous time; she would be too if she could join some pleasant group around a table and enjoy the program without having to make a spectacle of herself. If she didn't trip going up the steps, she'd probably fall off the platform when she saw the mike. With all the technology available, why couldn't someone invent a mike that couldn't poke a person in the nose? She'd be the wrong height to speak into it, and some helpful soul would rush forward to make an adjustment after she'd fumbled with it for a while, which would be all the delay she'd need to throw her into total panic.

Her directions had been to wait outside the ballroom. Because she didn't have a husband—ex-husbands being of no use at all—the conference committee had arranged for a vice-president from the company that published all her books to escort her to the stage when the award was announced. She'd never met the man, but

11

she appreciated the gesture. She was one romance writer with a dearth of flesh-and-blood men in her life. Her only sibling was a sister; her parents, quiet, retiring people themselves, were too overawed by her success to come to New York, and both her agent and editor were women.

Nearby, an author in gauzy yellow harem pants and a wide black belt was chatting with a striking blonde whose silky hair and green floor-length gown made Brenda feel like a country mouse. What'd happened to the "everyone wear pink" suggestion? Was she the only award winner who'd taken it seriously? Her pale cotton shirtdress had seemed just the thing for a breakfast affair when she'd bought it in Charlotte's best and only boutique, but in these surroundings it made her feel like a high school sophomore. Maybe they'd think she was an imposter; certainly there was nothing in her appearance to suggest that she wrote sensual, slightly racy romances. Unlike her heroines, who always had long tresses flowing down their backs, she wore her ebony-black hair pulled into a neat bun. She liked to give her creations dancing-emerald or honey-flecked brown eyes, not blue-gray like her own. Wearing heels, she was almost average height, but she described the women in her books as fragile and petite or willowy and model-slim. She never used her own finely molded, somewhat patrician features or oval face as a model for a heroine, preferring much more dramatic faces. She still thought her years of chubbiness in grade school had ruined her thighs, although her waist was small and the rest of her pleasantly proportioned.

Be logical, Brenda told herself sharply. Most of the people at the conference were nice, congenial women who looked like they'd be at home sipping coffee in her mother's kitchen. At twenty-nine she was one of the youngest successful authors. There wasn't one sound reason why she couldn't march up and accept her award with poise and confidence. The chances of stumbling, mumbling, or falling were practically nonexistent, and even her dress was all right for early spring daytime wear. She had enough natural color not to be washed out by pastels. Simple styles had always suited her, and she didn't really want to wear a satin evening gown in the morning, however glamorous someone else might look in one.

Unfortunately her own pep talk couldn't dry her sweaty palms or relax her tightly clenched jaw. Getting up in front of a group had paralyzed her since "show and tell" in kindergarten, and she'd been avoiding this kind of situation ever since.

"Brenda Storm?" A short, slightly balding man in a navy suit offered her his hand, and she took it gingerly, afraid he'd find hers clammy and guess how nervous she was. "I'm Clifford Fletcher, your escort."

"It's a pleasure to meet you, Mr. Fletcher," she said graciously, wondering why she could meet people easily on a one-to-one basis and still be petrified in front of a group.

Latecomers were still straggling into the ballroom, searching for the few seats that remained empty. Brenda glanced at badges, remembering that green hearts meant aspiring writers or fans, while the booksellers and possibly members of the press wore silver hearts on the bright pink cardboard rectangles.

"We're very proud of you," her escort from the publishing company was saying. "The other awards are rather arbitrary, but yours is based on sales alone. We're glad to have a bookseller like Eric Sheffield participating in the conference."

"Who's that?" she asked, not quite catching all that he said, her attention straying to a statuesque brunette

13

in a brick-red crepe dress, by far the most glamorous woman she'd seen at the conference so far.

"Eric Sheffield is the head of the bookstore chain giving you your award."

"Oh, sorry. I know who he is. I was asking about the woman in red over there."

"Nina Valjean. She's probably here to pick up another award for her art."

"Oh, a book-cover artist."

He must think I'm really out of it, she thought, straightening her belt, brushing a stray curl back from her forehead, and blotting her lips, even though she'd already nervously licked away most of her lip coloring.

The program was starting, and Brenda felt nothing but admiration for the conference's promoter; not only had she organized the gathering for hundreds of romance enthusiasts, she was able to stand in front of the huge crowd with a mike, even though she had to be exhausted by her responsibilities, and sound as if she were having a great time.

Fletcher checked his complicated digital watch. Was he as eager as she was to get the awards over with? Someone greeted the silky-haired blonde by name, identifying her as a historical writer Brenda admired. It would be great fun to meet authors whose books she'd read once this awards ordeal was over. She was being totally unreasonable resenting the acceptance speech she had to make, but she'd sure like to start enjoying the conference. Writing was sometimes a lonely profession for the only author of books in Charlotte, Illinois, and the opportunity to talk shop with her own peers had prompted her to sign up for the gathering even before she knew about the Sheffield award.

The preliminaries went much too fast, and the main business of the morning began with a flourish. According to the program she was still clutching in her hand like a security blanket, she would be the last winner to be presented. Historical writers fared well, and Brenda especially liked a husband and wife writing team who seemed to have a good sense of humor. Maybe when it was over she'd laugh at her own case of nerves, which was exactly what the best-new-author-of-the-year was doing in front of the mike, giving a clever thank-you speech that included some witty impressions of a small towner in New York City. Her description of the garbage workers who thought metal cans were musical instruments at 3 A.M. actually made Brenda chuckle, and she agreed with her escort when he suggested she leave her purse and program with a committee member he knew.

A man came onto the stage from the side, striding up to the mike, and Brenda knew her time was up. She was on a roller coaster with no way to get off until her terrifying ride was over. Could her escort sense how shaky she was? Pulling back her shoulders and sticking out her chin, she summoned all her courage, wondering distractedly why the feet in the neat gray pumps didn't seem to belong to her anymore.

The crowd was absolutely still, drinking in every word from the resonant male voice that had commandeered their attention.

"Eric always has the women eating out of his hand," Fletcher said, chuckling softly by her side, and it took her a minute to realize he was talking about Eric Sheffield, the head of the bookstores presenting her award.

". . . my great pleasure," he was saying, "to present Sheffield Bookshelves' award to the author who won the hearts of more readers than any other romance writer in the past year. You know," he went on in a more confidential tone, "I read the last Brenda Storm romance just to see what all the excitement's about, and it was a revelation to me. I think every man in the country

15

should read romances to find out how a woman likes to be loved."

The applause was thunderous, delaying her entrance and giving her a chance to really look at the company president who'd earned a reputation as a supersalesman as well as a company executive. From where she stood, still outside the ballroom, he looked average enough, neither short nor tall, his hair dark brown in a conventional cut, his suit a regulation businessman's beige, better tailored than the average man's but not especially distinctive. Except for his unusual warmth in speaking to the crowd, he appeared to be a moderately attractive, congenial person with no outstanding characteristics. As the hero of one of her books, he'd be hard to describe. "Nice" isn't a very meaty word.

"Brenda," he continued when the audience quieted, talking about her in an intimate tone that surprised her, since she'd never even met the man, "sold her first love story to *Sixteen Magazine* when she was only fifteen, writing steadily ever since. She's a professional all the way, publishing in local newspapers, teen-age publications, women's magazines, and even a few confessions before she discovered her potential in romance. After an early marriage right after high school and her divorce three years later, she worked her way through the University of Illinois solely by writing and has gone on to become the leading lady of romance in all five hundred and twenty-four Sheffield Bookshelves in the United States."

The blood was pounding in her temples. Whatever she'd expected, it wasn't such a personal introduction. He'd even mentioned her divorce! How could this man she'd never met casually spread her life and accomplishments out in front of an audience of strangers? Reason told her it was the price she had to pay for her success, but she felt so unbearably self-conscious she wanted to run from the room.

"Now," Fletcher whispered softly, offering his arm until she finally clutched at it.

The speaker was reciting a list of her books, seemingly from memory, as she slowly moved toward him on the arm of her escort. Giddy with nervousness, she was only vaguely aware of the bouquets of balloons suspended over every table, pinks, whites, and reds, with the strings weighted down by current romance releases. She was too intent on reaching the stage to notice the welcoming smiles on either side, wanting only to have done with her minute in the spotlight. Her foot was on the bottom step, Fletcher had taken away his arm, and the mike was looming ahead like the devil's pitchfork, waiting to impale her when another tremendous round of applause washed over her. She reached the microphone before realizing the people were clapping for her.

She'd imagined every possible disaster, but not even her hyperactive imagination would have conjured up a welcome like the one Eric Sheffield gave her. Putting his hands on her shoulders, he bent his head and kissed her thoroughly on her mouth, his lips lingering on hers long enough to bring whistles of encouragement from the audience.

"I wish all my duties were this enjoyable," he said, smiling, moving aside to make room for Brenda at the mike, lowering it with one smooth movement.

How wrong she'd been in her appraisal of him from the back of the ballroom. Nothing about Eric Sheffield was the least bit ordinary. His dark brown hair was the color of acorns in the fall, and his eyes were like polished walnut, reflecting like the surface of a finely oiled table. Taken separately, his features were only pleasingly regular, but the animation on his face gave him a devastating charm. He had the gift of concentrating so

17

fully on one person that Brenda felt alone with him in front of hundreds of people.

"I didn't expect a reward that nice," she quipped, amazed that she was able to joke about his kiss with a mike only inches from her face.

She remembered to thank her editor, her agent, her supportive family, and the people who'd organized the conference, and it was easy to express appreciation to the man who stood to the right of her, listening so attentively she might have been giving a modern version of the Gettysburg Address instead of a pat little acceptance speech. Surprising her again, he took over for Clifford Fletcher, walking her back through the ballroom, smiling and nodding responsively to women sitting at the tables.

"Thank you," she said awkwardly, backing away from him when he turned to face her outside the ballroom.

"You've already thanked me." He looked a little boyish when he grinned, and she wondered how old he was. "Are you staying for the whole conference?"

"I planned to, yes," she said.

"Good. Can you have lunch with me today?"

"I'd like to." That was an understatement! "But my agent, Madge Hastings, made arrangements to have lunch with another publisher. I shouldn't tell you that, I guess."

There was no reason to be secretive about talking to an editor from a rival publisher; she didn't have an exclusive contract. Still, she liked her editor, and her dealings with the company that had published all her books to date had been more than fair. She was talking to the representative from Heartstring Romances mainly to please her agent. Madge had sold her first book, helping her make it salable after several discouraging rejections; now her agent felt she wasn't earning her commission unless she shopped occasionally for a better deal. Brenda didn't think it was necessary, regarding Madge as a good friend as well as a business partner. Even though this was only the second time they'd met in person, she used their frequent phone conversations as a sounding board for the ideas and techniques developed in her books. Time spent with Madge was sure to be a highlight of her trip to New York.

"Your secret is safe with me, provided I get a raincheck," Eric said.

"Fine, if you want one."

"I have to rush. I'll be in touch."

He checked his watch and turned to go, looking much more like a harried businessman than he had on-stage. Of course, she'd probably never see him again, but she couldn't believe how gloomy that prospect made her feel.

He'd barely taken three steps when he came back to her.

"About kissing you . . ."

A black-banged young woman in a purple flowered top was observing the head of Sheffield Bookshelves with more than casual interest, and Brenda felt conspicuous, the heat of a blush rising to her cheeks.

"It doesn't matter," she said quickly.

"I was going to say I enjoyed it," he said a little less cordially, turning away and disappearing before she had a chance to explain.

What was there to explain? She couldn't tell a stranger that his casual kiss had made her forget her terror of public speaking long enough to get through her acceptance speech without stammering.

People were streaming out of the ballroom, hundreds of women with animated expressions on their faces and a scattering of men: husbands, representatives of publishing houses, agents, members of the press, and even a few male romance writers who wrote under female *noms de plume*. Brenda found herself moving with the flow until she remembered her purse and program. She had to fight her way against the crowd, slipping through wherever there was a small gap, until she found the worried-looking young woman who was still holding her purse.

"I was imagining you locked out of your hotel room, thinking I'd absconded with your bag," the committee person said, a grin softening her rather sharp features. "Congratulations on your award—or should I say awards? If kissing Eric Sheffield is one of the perks of being a romance writer, I'm going to lock myself in a tower and write until someone buys one of my manuscripts."

"There are rewards, but I'm not sure that's one of them," Brenda said doubtfully, taking her purse and looking at her program to see what came next. Her mind seemed to be a blank.

"Tell me the truth," the young woman urged. "You must have men trying to date you all the time to see if you're as sexy as the heroines in your books."

"No, it hasn't worked that way at all."

She didn't want to explain that the few eligible men in Charlotte, Illinois, were more intimidated than turned on by her success as a romance writer. One particularly attractive man who worked at the bank had even asked her why she didn't move someplace more exciting like Chicago or New York.

"You don't have to tell me," the young would-be writer teased. "As soon as I read that strip-poker scene between Cassandra and Ian in *Hasty Desire,* I knew you were one romance writer who knew what it was all about. I loved that scene! Actually I love all your books."

"It's really kind of you to say so. Thank you for holding my purse."

She backed away, then made a hasty retreat, never feeling really comfortable with fans, especially not when they praised her love scenes. No one seemed to believe that her torrid scenes were only exercises in imagination. True, she'd read *The Sensual Everything* and as many other books as she could find on modern sexuality, but she couldn't explain to strangers that the lovemaking in her books was wishful thinking, not experience. Marriage to Reilly Fenner had taught her a lot of things, but how to have fun in bed wasn't one of them. She knew now that he'd been insensitive, impatient, and selfish about his own satisfaction, but at the time she'd thought something was wrong with her. It'd never occurred to her ex-husband that she wasn't enjoying their relationship. So much for the amorous adventures of this romance writer, she thought with a trace of bitterness. Maybe she was still waiting for a dashing knight in shining armor to carry her off to his castle. Taking off that armor was never part of her favorite fantasy.

The crowd swept her along to the bank of elevators on the mezzanine. The rest of the morning would be devoted to a variety of workshops. Her preference was circled: a discussion on sensual writing led by an editor who was a pioneer in modern romances. She found the room, but so had a hundred or more other women, who now occupied all the available chairs and most of the standing room at the rear. Coming in behind the crowd, Brenda was hard-pressed to find a spot where she could see the speaker. After listening for ten minutes or so from a congested corner, she decided to circulate and see what was happening in other workshops.

A panel near the ballroom was discussing gothic romances. Even though their boom days were over for now, Brenda agreed with one speaker, who said there was always a market for the best; she loved to be scared and wondered if there was any way to use a gothic setting in one of her books. The habit of sifting through everything she heard for story ideas had become so ingrained, she hardly realized she was doing it. Some of her best ideas seemed to pop into her mind unexpectedly when, in fact, they'd been simmering in her subconscious for months or even years.

One thought that wouldn't stay submerged was the possibility of never seeing Eric Sheffield again. His part in the conference was over, and she didn't really believe he'd get in touch with her. She was sure his kiss had only been part of his performance for the audience, and she hated herself for remembering it so vividly. The tingling of her lips and the warm glow she felt were pure imagination, or else it had been too long since she'd enjoyed male companionship. She stopped following the train of conversation between the four panelists at the front of the room, who were mostly reviewing things she already knew. When there was a pause, she slipped away, deciding to return to her room and freshen up for lunch.

Her room, on a corridor to the right of the elevators on the ninth floor, was large by modern standards, with a double bed, two upholstered chairs, and standard hotel furnishings, but it was a disappointment after the gracefully aging lobby and ballroom. The charm of a bygone era hadn't survived as well in the sleeping accommodations, and she debated whether to report the drip in her shower. Since she couldn't hear it when the bathroom door was shut, she didn't. Confrontations with desk clerks were definitely on her list of undesirable contacts.

Maybe the brown-beige color scheme of the room had been chic thirty or forty years ago, but now it just seemed drab. The feature most pleasing to her was a window overlooking the street. Nocturnal garbage trucks notwithstanding, she loved to sit by the large screenless open window and look down on motorized traffic and pedestrians threading their way through the Manhattan maze. She could see more people in a few minutes than she did in five days in Charlotte, and she found herself especially watching for the mounted policemen. Horses were no novelty in rural Illinois, but the patient, well-trained law-enforcement beasts fascinated her. Where did a policeman learn to ride in New York City?

Her pleasure faded when she remembered that she'd have to snag a taxi for herself out of the parade of zigzagging yellow vehicles to get to her luncheon. New Yorkers made it look so easy: just step off the curb and raise your hand. If she didn't get clipped by a front bumper, she'd probably be ignored by the cab drivers.

The phone on the bed stand sounded, startling her into premonitions of disaster. No one in her family would call unless there was a major catastrophe, especially not while daytime rates were in effect, and who else could locate her in this hotel? She answered it, bracing herself for bad news.

"Brenda, it's Madge Hastings. How is the conference going?"

"Fine," she answered, brightening. "Our lunch date is for twelve thirty, isn't it?"

"Yes, but I was here anyway, so I thought I'd see if you're through for the morning."

"All done. You're in the hotel?"

"In the lobby."

"I'll be right down." Thank heavens, she wouldn't have to flag down a cab on her own!

Madge Hastings had red hair, sleekly styled in a short bob, and eyebrows tweezed to a narrow line. Once a fashion model, she was still chic and sophisticated, even

23

though her waist was thicker and her form more solid than in her modeling days. In her mid-forties, she looked her age but made her age look good. Unusually tall, she towered over Brenda, making her feel like part of a Mutt and Jeff team when they were standing. Madge snagged a cab quicker than a shortstop grabbing up a linedrive, whisking them off to a cozy little restaurant near the United Nations to meet the senior editor from Heartstring.

Fran Learner was nearly as tall as Madge and wore a dove-gray suit with a rose-petal-pink silk blouse. The outfit reminded her of one she'd seen in *Vogue*. Before buying her pink cotton dress, Brenda had read that pink and gray were the "in" colors for spring; the color of her dress was right but the style was definitely "out." Even though she anticipated receiving royalties later that year that could open the doors of high fashion, she felt like the poor country cousin of the two sophisticated women seated beside her.

The menu was written in French with English subtitles, but the waiter was impatient, slipping into the few inches of space between tables to take their order, his abruptness telling them he believed the myth that women were poor tippers. His attitude almost guaranteed small gratuities. Ninety percent of the tables had at least one man, but the editor and agent weren't the kind of women who slipped into discreet little department-store tearooms. Brenda enjoyed the power struggle between the waiter and her two companions, even though it didn't seem to have much to do with her. Fran invited her to order first, so she did, choosing a hearty veal dish she couldn't pronounce. One thing she wasn't shy about was eating, and, after being too nervous for breakfast, she was starved. She didn't regret her choice when Madge's skimpy spinach salad arrived, nor would she have traded her dish for the editor's cold vegetable

24

plate. She expected more for $8.95 than carrot sticks and marinated beans.

"I read *Hasty Desire* and enjoyed it very much," Fran said, signaling the end of their get-acquainted small talk.

"Thank you." Brenda was only halfway through the succulent morsels of buttery seasoned veal, but she felt an obligation to put her fork down and pay attention.

"We're working on a new line of longer, more sensual novels with emphasis on plot complications. We want to get away from the stereotyped themes."

Brenda thought her publisher was already doing that, but it would hardly do to point this out to the woman who was buying her the best luncheon she'd ever tasted. She couldn't resist picking up her fork and nibbling on another bit of veal, dipping it first into the savory sauce.

When her brother-in-law bargained for a new tractor to replace the one destroyed in the barn fire, he'd start talking prices first, and so would her mother when she bought merchandise to stock her small craft-supply business on Main Street. Brenda listened to words like "exclusive contracts," "royalty points," and "larger advances" with a skeptical ear, not hearing any mention of dollars. The editor reached into an oversized gray shoulder bag and handed her a writer's tip sheet, and suddenly Brenda remembered why the name Learner was familiar. Heartstring had rejected her first manuscript with a curt little note; she was sure this woman's name had been on the rejection slip.

Madge flashed a grin so brief it might have been imaginary, but Brenda read it correctly. The editor was bargaining with her hands tied. She really wasn't authorized to offer more than her company's standard contract. Brenda finished her meal, buttering a last fragment of hard-crusted bread, listening attentively but without real interest. It would take more than lunch and vague benefits to woo her away from a company that had treated her fairly and encouraged her when she needed it. In spite of her imaginative approach to writing, she was still her father's daughter, and the practical lessons she'd learned helping in his hardware store stuck.

Could she be this practical if she fell in love again? What would it take to make her risk giving her heart to someone for the second time? Sipping at her water and pretending interest in the rival editor's sophisticated spiel, she thought about Eric Sheffield, wondering what he really thought of the author who'd won his company's award. Had he expected someone more exotic, like the woman in harem pants or the lovely cover artist in the red dress? Had he planned to kiss the award-winning author even if she'd been horse-faced with a wart on her nose? Both of the women sitting with her were as tall or taller than he, she noted, but any satisfaction that gave her was short-lived. A man with his self-confidence would date anyone who pleased him, regardless of height, and in this city every other woman was stiff competition. Date! She didn't even know if he was married. Attractive men almost always were.

"Were you surprised when you learned you'd received the award from Sheffield?" Fran was asking.

"Yes," Brenda answered, shaking off her daydreaming mood. "I was surprised Eric Sheffield gave it to me in person too."

"Why shouldn't he?" Madge asked, pretending she hadn't just checked her watch, hoping the editor would get to the point soon or shut up. "He's gotten rich selling romances, and he's smart enough to know that women readers keep his stores in business."

"Yes, I suppose so," Brenda agreed.

"I met him at a party," Fran said. "He was with

26

Katherine Belding, the star of *Longing for Life*. What a marvelous film that was. I saw it in . . ."

"He's not married?" Brenda interrupted.

"No, he's that rare breed, a completely unattached male. Oh, I brought a copy of a book we're particularly proud of," the editor said, switching the topic and digging into her bag again. "It'll be in the stores in about three weeks, but I'd love to have you read it and give me your reaction. This is the closest we've come yet to our ideal romance."

Brenda thanked her for the lunch and book, glad that the meeting was over. Madge had an appointment, but she told Brenda she'd see her at the conference later that afternoon. She also promised Fran Learner they'd talk more later, although Brenda could have saved her the trouble with a simple "no thanks."

Both women offered to share a cab with her, but she declined, welcoming the long walk back to the hotel to work off her lunch, see more of the city, and sort out disturbing feelings about the award and the man who'd presented it.

CHAPTER TWO

On her way through the lobby Brenda stopped at the desk and asked if she had any messages, then felt silly for doing it. In her whole life no one had ever left a message for her with a hotel clerk, and only wishful thinking made her hope Eric Sheffield had tried to contact her.

Inside her room, she stared down moodily at the midday traffic, not even bothering to glance at the rows of windows in the bulky building across the street. One of her favorite pastimes was trying to imagine a story taking place behind unfamiliar facades, picturing a room and peopling it with all kinds of fascinating characters. Right now her own life was too absorbing for games of make-believe.

She was wasting her day. The conference she'd anticipated so keenly was going on without her, and one of the world's most colorful cities was right at hand. How could she idly mope around in her room? Catching sight of herself in the dresser mirror, she made one decision. No way would she wear her demure little cotton dress for another minute, pink or no pink. Just to make sure she couldn't change her mind, she impatiently undid the little pearly buttons, slipped out of it, and wadded it into the bottom of her suitcase, where it could gather wrinkles until she got back to Illinois. Opening the wooden door of the big, high-ceilinged closet, she was thankful for once that she always overpacked, bringing twice what she needed because she was never quite sure what to wear. The morning session had been like a costume party, with everything from a period gown to polyester slacks. She'd be more inconspicuous trying to be conspicuous than she would dressing like a country cousin.

Still standing in her lacy white slip in front of the closet, she was startled by a loud rap on the door. Dashing to the tiny peephole, she peered out, getting a distorted glimpse of Eric Sheffield, his forehead ballooning out like an image in a fun-house mirror. Sure that the pounding of her heart was drowning out her voice, she called out, "Just a minute," and frantically scrambled for something to wear, knocking three empty hangers to the floor as she grabbed for a garment.

She had it buttoned from top to bottom before wondering why on earth she'd chosen her raincoat, a tailored, belted tan coat perfectly suitable for outdoor wear on spring days but silly for greeting someone in her room. Another knock kept her from changing into something more appropriate; the man wouldn't wait forever.

"Oh, you're just going out," he said cordially. "Glad I caught you."

She moved backward into the room, taking tiny little steps so her coat wouldn't open and reveal her slip underneath.

"Actually I just got back." This was somewhat true.

"Let me take your coat."

What was he doing playing host in her room?

"Oh, no! I mean, no thank you. I opened the win-

29

dow." The darn thing was open only three inches. "It's cool in here."

If it was so cool, why was a light film of perspiration forming above her upper lip? He closed the door and sat on the edge of the double bed, so totally at home she felt like a marionette, unable to move unless someone pulled a string.

"I was hoping to catch you before the hospitality rooms opened this afternoon."

"That's not for another hour." She was guessing, not even sure she still knew how to tell time. Eric Sheffield was impressive enough on a stage, basking in the admiration of hundreds of women. Alone with him in a hotel room, she felt as if a movie star had stepped off the screen, materializing as a real human being. This man wasn't handsome like a screen idol, but his self-assurance, his grace and openness hit her like a meteorite shower, making her realize she'd never adequately described a hero in any of her books. Charisma wasn't something that could be easily described with words. Or was she overreacting because he'd saved her from making a fool of herself with her acceptance speech?

"How did your luncheon go?" he asked, looking at her so intently she suspected him of practicing hypnotism.

"Fine. I mean, it was interesting, but I really am happy with the publisher I have."

Once a professor had made her list one hundred descriptive words that could be used in place of "interesting." What a time to forget all of them! She kept her eyes on his necktie, a plain but expensive-looking brown with a sword symbol done in gold thread.

"I'd like to take you to dinner tonight, if it won't interfere with your plans."

Her only plan had been to follow the agenda for the conference so she wouldn't miss a thing. At this moment she couldn't remember a single activity listed on her program.

"I don't know—that is, I can't remember what's scheduled for tonight."

She inched her way carefully to her purse, with tiny steps so the coat wouldn't gape open, and extracted the agenda from under it, pretending to read. The words swam across the page, and she knew she'd skip whatever was planned even if the Prince and Princess of Wales were supposed to be her dinner companions.

He looked a little skeptical as she rustled the sheaf of papers, and it wasn't hard to guess that women didn't often hesitate in accepting his invitations.

"You won't miss anything crucial, will you?"

"No, I'll be glad to have dinner with you."

Was that calm, decisive voice really hers? The world lost a great actress when she flunked "show and tell."

"Fine."

No man should be allowed to use a smile like his without a notice pinned on his jacket: WARNING, CLOSE VISUAL CONTACT MAY BE HAZARDOUS TO YOUR HEART.

"How does the Rainbow Room sound? I made a reservation for eight."

"Eight people?" Her brain cells were definitely short-circuiting! "Eight o'clock?"

"Shall I meet you in the lobby here, say at seven thirty? It's only a couple of blocks away. I flew here and haven't bothered to rent a car yet, so we can catch a cab."

"I like to walk, but don't you live here?"

"Do I sound like a New Yorker?" He grinned.

"No, I guess not." He was so smooth, he didn't seem to belong to any region.

"Our headquarters is in Minneapolis."

"You must have grown up in the Midwest to live in the snow belt."

He frowned and she felt diminished. "You're still in Illinois."

"I grew up in Charlotte."

"I grew up in Hendersonville, Wisconsin. Ever hear of it?"

" 'Fraid not."

"I started my first bookstore while I was at the University of Wisconsin. Used texts and paperbacks. I figured it beat waiting on tables to get through college. I never saw any reason to move my main office out of the Midwest."

"So you're an entrepreneur." She hoped she'd pronounced it right; it wasn't a word she said aloud very often.

"With quite a bit of help from my grandfather. He was impressed because I didn't let my parents pay my way."

He rested his palms on his knees, not looking at all inclined to leave. Still standing by the dresser, fiddling with the conference program, she kept her eyes riveted on his feet, clad in dark brown wing-tip shoes with socks almost the same color.

"Do you ski?" he asked after a pause that seemed to last longer than it did.

"Yes, in an amateur sort of way. I have a cousin who manages a ski resort near Gaylord, Michigan. I try to get up there once every winter. Her daughters are only eight and ten, but they ski like little champions. I just plod along on the easy slopes."

All her cousins were female too. Reilly used to complain that the deck was stacked against him in getting sons, but he'd never seriously wanted to start a family. It would've meant growing up himself, she realized now.

32

"We have a few good runs in Minnesota too."

Why did everything he said sound like an invitation?

"So I've heard."

"Don't you want to take your coat off?"

Some of the love scenes she wrote embarrassed her mother. How could she be too prudish to tell him she was wearing only a slip?

"I was changing when you knocked," she forced herself to admit.

"I wondered about that pink dress. But don't let me stop you if you want to change."

"I'm not in that much of a hurry!"

"But you're not mad?" He grinned winningly.

She wasn't.

"They were urging everyone to wear pink the first morning. It was the best I could find in Charlotte."

"Don't apologize. You looked like an adorable Barbie Doll."

"A Barbie Doll! I wasn't apologizing."

What did he know about little girls' toys? She didn't ask but he told her anyway.

"My daughter loves Barbies. She must have twenty, all dressed in clothes she made herself. That's my subtle way of telling you I'm divorced and have a child."

"How old is she?"

"Eleven. She lives with her mother, stepfather, and two little half brothers in St. Paul. Spends most of the summer with me. Am I telling you more than you want to know?"

"No, not at all," she admitted, relaxing because he was the kind of person who seemed like an old friend on short acquaintance.

"What else can I tell you?"

She met his eyes and found a warm invitation there.

"How old are you?"

33

"Thirty-seven going on seventy, according to my ex-wife. That's only to warn you, I have one glaring fault."

"Oh?" It certainly wasn't a visible one; he radiated good health.

"I'm a workaholic, and much as I'd like to stay here, I have an appointment across town in seventeen minutes. If there's an elevator waiting on this floor and a cab right outside the door, I have thirty-two seconds to spare. How would you like to spend them?"

"This morning I waited five minutes for an elevator with enough room for me to get in."

"Rush-hour crowd. I feel luckier than that." He walked over to her, lightly brushed his lips against her forehead, and went to the door. "Very lucky."

After he'd left she held her fingers over the spot he'd kissed, befuddled by the effect he had on her. Twice she'd seen him and twice he'd kissed her. Was he a supercharged Casanova type or just a natural toucher? Was he too much for her to handle or too nice to be real? Nothing she'd learned about men in Charlotte, Illinois, gave her the slightest clue.

Her gray gabardine jacket and matching skirt were sold in a hundred thousand retail stores across the country, including one in Charlotte, but she felt less conspicuous in a suit with a crisp white cotton blouse. Pale hose hadn't caught on in her hometown, but wearing them here she blended into the crowd on the second floor, where rooms were available for conference gatherings. She felt almost invisible in the milling crowd, which was just how she wanted to feel.

Each romance publisher had a hospitality room with editors as hosts and hostesses. Brenda moved at a leisurely pace, stopping at each one, gathering up writers' tip sheets, sample books, and publicity handouts but bypassing the tables loaded with *hors d'oeuvres* and beverages. After her rich and filling lunch she wouldn't let herself indulge in midday snacking. Each room had its own atmosphere. One publisher of gaudy-covered historicals used oversized posters and balloons for a carnival decor, while another proffered fancy tidbits on silver trays with white linen on the tables. Heartstring's editor was surrounded by a group of aspiring writers, and Brenda passed through that room quickly. Let her agent take care of business; she was there to have fun.

Several people started conversations with her, surprising her by remembering even her earlier books. In a business with literally hundreds of writers struggling for recognition, it was gratifying to know that readers really noticed who wrote their favorite type of literature. Madge was nowhere in sight, but it didn't really matter. Brenda had a three-book contract to fill in the next six months, but she needed a break from writing; she didn't want to start thinking about her next book until her vacation in New York was over.

Her own publisher's room was at the end of a corridor, perhaps for that reason escaping the heaviest concentration of people. The whole editorial staff was there, all their names were familiar to her, but she'd met her own editor only once before this. Unlike some rooms where one or more men sat behind a table and seemed to preside over the activity, this one was hosted only by four women, the senior editor and her staff. Brenda had spotted a number of writers who were in their forties or older, but most romance editors were younger career women, poised and assertive in their responsible jobs. The romance book industry was a new one in the United States, booming on the scene only a few years ago, built from scratch by talented women. Brenda had never felt more excited about being a part of romance publishing, not even when she'd seen her first book in a bookstore.

Her editor introduced her to several other writers, a

35

special pleasure because she'd always felt the authors writing for this house were part of a team. Her own first book had sold well because the romances preceding it had appealed to readers. Every time a reader enjoyed another book in her publisher's line, it increased her chances of selling her next book. The last thing she wanted to do was write for three different companies using four or five pen names. She decided to be firm with Madge; no more shopping around for different publishers. Her best bet now was to write as many books as possible, trying to make each one better than the last. It occurred to her, not for the first time, that she probably didn't need an agent anymore. But once she'd needed her a great deal, and she wasn't likely to forget that.

"I caught up with you!"

Madge didn't come into a room, she made an entrance. Brenda admiringly envied her statuesque grace; just once she'd like to burst into a room and look down on everyone in it, but she'd probably break her neck on stilts.

"I was just thinking about you," Brenda said truthfully enough.

"I finally pinned Learner down on royalties. She's talking six on the first hundred thousand and eight after that. I told her no chance."

"Good," Brenda said, distracted from the discussion of royalty percentage points by a glimpse of dark brown hair and a beige suit in the corridor.

The man turned, showing her a deeply tanned face with a finely chiseled Roman nose and a high brow. He was more handsome than the man she'd hoped to see, but there was no special glow on his face. Was she only imagining Eric Sheffield's uniqueness? Maybe after she spent a whole evening with him, he'd seem more like an ordinary man.

Leaving the hospitality rooms with plenty of time to spare, she did everything to herself that could be done in a hotel room: bathing, shampooing, manicuring, powdering, primping, and making up with special care. She brushed her hair forward over one side of her face for a more sultry look, but decided it just wasn't her style and whisked it back into the usual bun. After applying the bright-red lipstick she wore only on red-letter occasions, she changed her mind about that too and blotted it off. Eric might see her as a Barbie Doll, but she'd be a tastefully dressed one.

She'd brought the dressiest dress in her wardrobe, a black crepe with tight sleeves that hugged her wrists and came to a point on the top of her hand. Putting on her black bra, panties, and slip made her feel exotic, but zipping up the dress in front of a mirror planted a nagging little doubt in her mind. With a high neckline and a narrow fabric belt above the straight skirt, it seemed more severe than it had when she bought it. Worse, she'd forgotten the showy rhinestone jewelry she usually wore to brighten it and had to settle for a thin gold chain and black onyx earrings. Her silver evening slippers, uncomfortable as they were, probably would've looked better than the practical suede pumps she was wearing, but they were home in a box on her closet shelf.

She had a terrible habit of getting ready early, leaving herself nothing to do but pace and fidget. How she envied her sister, who never got ready for anything without a frantic last-minute rush. Julie never had time to worry whether she was overdressed or underdressed.

Throwing caution to the wind, she decided to leave her raincoat behind. She couldn't imagine feeling cold in Eric's company and refused to worry about the weather. Were five minutes enough to get to the lobby? She probably could walk down nine flights in less than that, but she wanted to allow for pokey elevators. Her white gold watch didn't match, so she left it on the dresser, checking it one last time before leaving her room. A genuine European prince was going to escort one lucky conference goer to the closing banquet; Brenda felt as if she'd already won the drawing for the most romantic date.

So excited she could have floated down without an elevator, she had to wait and wait and wait for one to finally stop. What if he didn't come? She might wait alone in the lobby for ages. If he wasn't there, how long should she stand there? This worry changed to anxiety about being late as the elevator stopped on the seventh, sixth, and fifth floors, picking up lodge brothers who were too wrapped up in getting acquainted with each other to push the DOOR CLOSE button and speed their descent.

Eric was waiting, watching the elevators opening and shutting in front of him. His masterfully tailored charcoal suit was a sign of his sophistication, but he didn't seem as self-contained this evening, shifting his weight first to one foot, then the other, adjusting his tie against the stark white of his shirt before he saw her.

The lobby clock said 7:42, and he glanced at it before moving toward her. Steaming at the lengthy elevator ride, since she was never tardy for anything, Brenda tried to smile a casual greeting but felt more like bawling. She knew how Cinderella would have felt if she hadn't gotten a single smile from the prince before everything dissolved into a jumble of rags, mice, and chunks of pumpkin.

"I thought maybe you were waiting for me in your room," he said.

"No, I thought you said the lobby."

"I did."

"The elevator was slower than I expected. I'm sorry."

Were those few minutes going to ruin the evening? He seemed to have a thing about promptness.

"No problem." He smiled, finally. "Maybe we can get a cab."

Seventeen lodge brothers had the same idea, creating a minor traffic jam as they debated with a cab driver about how many passengers could fit in one vehicle. A second taxi had been commandeered by the same group, and two weren't enough to handle the fraternal party.

"Not very promising," Eric said with a trace of irritation.

"I really like to walk," she assured him. "This is the warmest evening so far this spring."

"If you're sure you don't mind . . ."

He touched her arm lightly to indicate their direction, then started to cross the intersection just as the DO NOT WALK warning flashed. Hesitating, then stopping, she hung back instead of following him; she just didn't have what it took to walk against signals, even when traffic was light. From the other side of the street, he turned back to glance at her, waiting on the far curb. She debated whether to make a run for it against the light, but her common sense won out.

"Thought I'd lost you," he joked when she caught up.

"Sorry."

"Don't be. You're the law-abiding citizen."

Measured in blocks, the walk was short, but her misgivings grew with every step. He was so quiet! Had she only imagined his charm? Certainly he couldn't be mad just because she'd been a little late!

Not until they were alone in an express elevator speeding toward the top floor of the RCA building did her misgivings begin to seem unfounded.

"You look lovely tonight," he said softly.

"Thank you."

It was what she wanted to hear, so why did she feel let down? His compliment pleased her, but she worried that he didn't mean it. It was a conventional thing to say, and she wanted to feel special, to mean something to him. But, of course, her fertile imagination was working overtime again, anticipating something that would never happen. He'd only asked her out to be courteous; he had a free evening away from home, so he was entertaining his company's award winner. Sudden romance was the stuff that sold books; she was much too old to expect anything like it in her own life. Maybe they wouldn't even like each other after an evening together.

The wall ahead was a black mirror, barely reflecting the pale image of her face and making her feel like Alice in a tunnel to Wonderland. A *maître d'* in formal wear took Eric's name, checked his reservations list, and escorted them up a few steps into an elegant room. Their table by the window looked out over a fabulous panorama of the city, and she didn't care if she gawked like a tourist. It was just dark enough for the city lights to be dotting the skyline, and she wanted to press her nose to the glass to see all of it.

A waiter who reminded her of an Italian opera star took their drink order, bringing white wine for her and scotch and water for Eric. By the time they ordered rack of lamb for two, an orchestra was playing mellow dance music.

"Would you like to dance?" For the first time that evening he turned the full force of his smile on her, and she would have parachuted out the window if he'd asked.

"I'd love to."

The dancing area wasn't large, and Eric held her close, taking small steps and guiding her with a firm hand on her waist. She'd rarely danced this way. Reilly liked to polka, and trying to follow his long-legged bounce used to make her teeth rattle.

"This is nice," she said, loving the touch of his hand on hers. "The music, I mean."

"The music?" He pulled her closer, his chin just above the top of her head.

He smelled delicious, clean and spicy, and his fingers caressed her wrist, turning her insides to marshmallow.

"Our dinner will be coming," he said at the end of a number, leading the way back to the table.

"I'm a little rusty, I guess," she murmured.

"I didn't notice."

He pulled out a chair and seated her, then sat down across from her.

"I guess we're doing what the tourists do," he said.

How many tourists went dining and dancing with a fascinating stranger? She tried to think of something clever or humorous to say, but a little kernel of apprehension made her tongue-tied. He sipped his ice water but didn't turn his head to gaze down on the city. At least he seemed to like looking at her.

"It's quite a view," he said, his eyes still on her.

"Yes, it is." Her eyes met his, then quickly flitted to the light-studded view. "Do you come here often?"

"To New York? A few times a year."

"It must be quite a responsibility, running your company."

He laughed unexpectedly. "Quite a responsibility. And the weather is fine, the view is great, and if we're lucky, the food will be good. Now let's talk about something we're really interested in. Do you live by yourself?"

"Yes, in a bungalow on the outskirts of Charlotte. Do you?"

"Yes."

"In Minneapolis?"

41

"On a lake about forty-five minutes from the city. Easy commuting distance."

"That sounds nice."

Nice! Where were all her colorful adjectives when she needed them? He'd think she was hopelessly dull!

The waiter brought their dinners, serving the lamb from a cart beside the table, artistically arranging the small chops in a setting of firm, colorful vegetables, placing the plates in front of them with a flourish. Brenda sipped at her wine, playing with a few drops on her tongue and watching Eric from beneath lowered lashes. He cut a small bite, holding it on his fork while his eyes searched her face.

"Mr. Sheffield, it's awfully nice of you to bring me here, but you don't need to feel obligated. I mean, just because I won your company's award—I mean . . ."

"Eric."

"What?"

"Call me Eric. It is my name."

"Yes, of course, Eric. I just don't want you to feel stuck with me all evening."

"Why would I feel stuck?"

"I just . . ." Her voice trailed off, and she tried to disguise her confusion by breaking off a sliver of carrot with her fork and putting it into her mouth. She'd had dates go sour before, but this one seemed especially important. She felt foolish, wanting so much yet expecting so little. What did she have in common with a dynamic owner of a bookstore chain?

"Dinner with me isn't part of the award, if that's what you're thinking." He softened his reprimand with a warm smile.

She sliced a morsel of lamb, hating the awkward way she felt. "You must have an awfully busy schedule, being responsible for five hundred and twenty-four bookstores."

42

"I always leave time in my schedule for pleasure. There's not a thing I have to do until eight fifty-seven tomorrow morning when my flight leaves for Toronto. But I'm thinking of canceling my reservation."

"Oh?" She raised her brows, unconsciously covering the lower part of her face with her hand.

"Do you want to know why?" he asked.

Impatient with her own feeling of unease, she put both hands on her lap, forgetting about the meal. "If you want to tell me."

"I'm debating whether to cancel my trip because I think it's going to take more than a few hours to convince you to spend the next three weeks with me."

Startled, she wasn't sure whether to be angry or elated. "I'm not that grateful for the award!" She didn't intend to snap, but his suggestion floored her.

He quickly reached across the table and caught her hand in his. "Hear me out. I never thought you were. I have a simple business proposition for you. Eat your dinner. It's getting cold."

"So is yours. What kind of business?" She didn't try to hide her suspicion.

"A promotional tour of some of my larger stores. Autograph parties, newspaper interviews, TV appearances, whatever my local managers can drum up to publicize the award and your new book."

What she really wanted to hear was the part about spending three weeks with him.

"I don't know."

"Let's eat," he urged, finally smiling with real warmth.

The meal was too good to abandon, but she was much more interested in the tour of his stores.

"I plan to rent a car and work my way back to Minneapolis, stopping at stores along the way. There's no reason why you can't come with me."

"There are several." She was trying hard to think of some.

"Oh?"

"I have a book to write."

"I'm sure your publisher will give you an extension, since this is a publicity tour."

She didn't really need one; she worked fast when deadlines pressured her.

"Three weeks is a long time."

She meant three weeks with him was a long time.

"Not so long. You'll be busy."

"Surely you can't arrange television appearances on such short notice."

Please, no TV, no mikes, no cameras, she wanted to say.

"Watch me."

"When did you think of this?"

"While I was waiting for you in the lobby."

"It's just an impulse, then. You're not serious."

"I'm very serious. It's the best plan I've come up with for selling books and seeing more of you."

"I really can't go, Eric."

It was her common sense talking; the last thing she needed was a frantic trip filled with public appearances. No, even if she could handle that, she couldn't travel with this man. She wasn't the kind of person who could enjoy a fling. It was safer to do without romance than to risk rejection after a no-strings affair.

"I knew two hours wouldn't be enough time. I'm going to call the airport."

He had time to make more than one call while the waiter cleared their plates, bringing the frosty after-dinner drinks he'd told her to order. Her grasshopper was nearly gone before Eric returned.

"It's settled. I got someone else to go to the meeting in Toronto."

"You shouldn't have canceled your trip."

If he assumed he could talk her into it, he hadn't met a stubborn woman before.

"Let's dance."

"Eric, I want you to understand that it's out of the question. I can't take three weeks off."

"You're the only romance writer I've met who looks like one of her heroines."

"My heroines always have blond or red hair."

"Oh? Don't you imagine yourself living a romantic life?" He was standing, waiting for her to get up from her chair.

"I write fiction," she said coolly.

"Isn't fiction a reflection of real life?"

She stood, keeping the chair between them.

"Not my real life," she said emphatically.

"I think you could use this setting in one of your books."

She probably would. Elegant dining in Charlotte meant going to a spaghetti dinner at the Elks on Friday night, but she wasn't going to tell him that. Her parents had probably danced together as teen-agers in the high school gym to the number the orchestra was playing, but it was melodious, inviting her to relax in Eric's arms.

He whispered into her hair, telling her she was lovely, drawing her closer until she felt like melting against his hard chest. Their feet were barely moving when he slid his hand to the back of her neck, bending to brush her lips with his when she looked up at him.

Brenda couldn't believe how natural it felt to be in Eric's arms. It should take weeks or even months to feel so comfortable with a man. But darn it, nothing like this would ever happen to her at home! Was it so terrible to pretend that this was real just for a few hours?

Closing her eyes, she surrendered herself to the music

45

and his gentle lead, knowing she'd written dozens of times about the delicious sensation of being infatuated with a handsome man, without adequately describing how she felt at this moment.

She couldn't succumb to his obvious charm! The man was cooking up some scheme to have her spend three weeks with him. If his intentions didn't spell disaster, then she'd better retire her imagination.

The number ended, and she made a lame excuse to leave the restaurant. Outside cooler air was washing over the city, making her welcome his closeness as he put his arm around her shoulder.

"Where would you like to go?"

"I'd just like to walk for a while," she suggested, loving the liveliness of the city streets. The pleasant weather seemed to have brought people into the open, and she didn't feel at all apprehensive about being out after dark, not when so many others seemed to be strolling arm in arm or hand in hand.

They didn't talk much as they walked on sidewalks with darkened buildings towering on all sides. When they reached Times Square he didn't seem to mind her playing tourist, staring at sleazy nightspots and the dazzling confusion of billboards and signs. In their short walk they passed enough electronic shops to keep the whole country in music, and she wondered about the New York City tendency to group the same kind of shops together. There seemed to be a section for everything from fish and vegetables to jewelry and furniture. The few supermarkets she'd passed in cabs looked about a tenth the size of the Charlotte supermarket. Where did eight million people buy their groceries? Even those in residential areas seemed dinky.

How many men would let her soak up atmosphere without feeling compelled to keep up a continual barrage of small talk? Maybe, in different circumstances, with more time to become acquainted . . .

She couldn't let herself dream about romance. They were ships passing in the night. No! How could she even think such a trite phrase? They were two people thrown together by fate. Worse! She'd never think of a good way to describe their evening if he didn't stop sliding his hand lower on her back.

For once don't worry about describing something, she told herself angrily. Just enjoy the evening!

They strolled up the street, stepping around street merchants who exhibited an incredible array of goods, clothing, electronic equipment, sunglasses, imported novelties, and pure junk on the pavement, even at this time of night. A person could easily have a six-course meal from all the mobile food sellers hawking hot dogs, chestnuts, oriental tidbits, cold drinks, candy, and a variety of other edibles. Tight economic times seemed to have turned the city streets into one huge bazaar.

The wind was brisker and cooler now, and she shivered a little in spite of Eric's arm around her back.

"You're cold. I'd better get a cab."

She wanted to say she'd willingly spend the whole night wandering with him, turning corners and exploring new streets, soaking up the rich ambiance of the city. At home she knew every person who passed her little house during the day, and she could set her clock by the math teacher who always jogged by at 5:15 or the woman next door who walked her poodle at 7:20. Seeing so many people at once was a treat to her senses; so was the nearness of Eric, his arm holding her protectively close so she could catch the spicy scent of his after-shave and feel the firmness of his hip when it brushed against her.

He flagged a taxi, although she expressed her willingness to walk back to the Roosevelt. Sliding in beside her, he gave the driver the name of her hotel, and she began to believe again that their date had been just a casual courtesy extended to her. She'd probably been reading things into the evening that hadn't even occurred to him. He might think it was good for business to have her tour his bookstores, but it was unlikely he had any personal interest in her.

"I'll get out alone at my hotel so you can keep the cab to go to yours," she suggested.

"No, I'll see you in."

His arm was behind her, his fingers just brushing the top of her shoulder.

"Are you cold now?" he asked.

"No. Well, maybe just a little."

She was inviting him to hug her, but he didn't need an invitation to search out her lips and cover them with his. As kisses went, his were spectacular, consuming her mouth, making her tingle with excitement. The ride to the Roosevelt was much too short. Where were the traffic jams when she wanted them?

"You don't have to come in," she reluctantly assured him as he paid the driver, trying not to admit to herself that she'd be crushed if he didn't.

"No, but I want to."

He took her arm as they approached the inside stairs to the lower arcade level, holding it while they climbed the short flight to the lobby.

"Would you like a drink?"

"All right," she agreed, moving toward the lounge and bar at the rear of the hotel lobby, climbing another short flight of steps.

They found a small table in a corner, and Eric went to the bar to buy drinks. A woman with curly ash-blond hair was seated at the bar, talking in a loud, giggly voice with two young men who looked like athletes killing time between games. They were teasing her about her

48

romances, trying to talk the writer into giving them "samples." The woman, vaguely familiar from the conference, seemed to be enjoying herself, but she was making Brenda uncomfortable. Did all men think a romance writer was an easy mark? Did Eric think so? His idea for a tour had been a spur-of-the-moment thought, as he'd readily admitted. If she went with him, would she find it was only a pretense? Was he interested in sleeping with her, not promoting her?

"You're sure all you want is soda?" he asked, setting an undersized cola bottle and a glass in front of her.

"Yes. I've never seen such a small bottle."

"For three dollars you'd think they'd give you a regular size," he said, sitting down beside her.

"Three dollars for a tiny cola! That's terrible!"

"Rent on this space," he teased, "although you don't take up that much."

Sipping his scotch and water, he watched her closely, making her more uncomfortable with each passing minute.

"Your new book," he said, "the one you're just starting. What's it about?"

"The usual." Talking about unhatched ideas always made her uncomfortable. She was afraid the plot would sound dumb if she described it aloud. "Woman meets man. Courtship."

"There was more than that in the book I read."

"I try to tell a good story."

"Some parts were very good."

She braced herself, sure that he'd refer to her love scenes.

"Your dialogue especially. You had me laughing out loud in that scene in the theater."

This was praise she really appreciated.

"Thank you. You did read it, then?"

"Skeptical wench! Yes, I did read it, and I did like it."

49

His tone told her he hadn't expected to. His hand was telling her something too, fondling her knee where her skirt had inched up under the table. If he mentioned a single bedroom scene, she'd make a run for the fire stairs.

She finished her three-dollar cola, feeling torn between wanting to sit with him all night and not wanting him to follow her to her room. When he offered another, she refused.

"We have a full schedule tomorrow starting with breakfast," she explained.

"When can I see you again?"

"There are workshops, then a luncheon."

"You'll give some serious thought to a promotional tour?"

"Eric, I don't think . . ."

"Just agree to consider it."

"I don't want to mislead you."

"You aren't."

In the lobby she began to thank him for dinner.

"I'll see you to your room." He followed her into an elevator that opened too quickly for her to argue. "What floor?"

It wasn't terribly flattering that he'd forgotten her room number. "Nine."

They were alone in the elevator, but he watched her from the opposite side, making her feel like a butterfly under the observation of a collector.

"Well, thank you . . ." she tried again, but he got off with her, asking for her key.

They were in front of her door before she managed to extract it from the small evening bag. He took it without giving her a chance to protest.

"I'm not coming in," he said, pushing open the door to let her pass into the room. "For long."

She was sure he shouldn't come in at all, but the

50

protest died in her throat as his mouth found hers. She was dimly aware of the door clicking shut, then his arms were around her, locking her against him as his lips made hers throb. He reached up and cupped her ears with his hands, letting his fingers play through her silky hair, gently brushing his lips over her forehead, across her closed lids, down to the tip of her nose.

"No," she said, trying to convince herself that she meant it.

"All right," he whispered, releasing her but keeping her close to him with a warm, liquid gaze that crumbled her resistance. "Think about the tour, darling. I think it would be very right for both of us."

He was gone before she could react to his words, but his intentions were painfully clear. He wanted a playmate on his trip back to Minnesota, and how could she be more convenient? He wouldn't even have to go much out of his way to drop her off in Illinois when his fun was over. Well, Mr. Eric Sheffield was going to find out that her profession didn't make her a pushover. She was one woman who still had to be wooed and won. And if her determination faltered, she could picture a TV interviewer pushing a mike in her face while a camera recorded her stark terror. Imagine having to face that day after day, town after town! The bookseller's persuasiveness wasn't enough to launch her on a marathon string of public appearances. She hoped.

CHAPTER THREE

She hadn't requested a wake-up call; her own little travel alarm was set for 7:30, leaving plenty of time to get ready for the breakfast meeting. Groping for the receiver, she nearly knocked the heavy old-style phone off the stand, but she wasn't too sleepy to notice it wasn't quite seven o'clock.

"Hello," she mumbled, sure that she was getting someone else's early morning summons.

"Good morning. It's Eric. Did I wake you?"

"Sort of," she admitted, propelled to full wakefulness by the mellow tone of his words. Even if she'd never seen him, she'd still melt hearing his throaty, resonant voice.

"Sorry."

"No, don't be. My alarm should ring any second now."

"I'm still in bed myself."

No, no, don't tell me that, she wanted to say, unable to suppress an image of his head on a white pillowcase, hair unruly and lids still heavy with sleep. How would it feel to wake up beside that face, to feel his soft kisses before she was fully conscious? It wasn't fair for his

52

voice to make her feel all warm and woozy this way. In the light of day, her nighttime fantasies about him made her uncomfortable.

"Oh." What could she say?

"Before I get dressed, I want to know if you'll have breakfast with me?"

Did he wear pajamas in bed? She liked to dress her heroes in silk ones, pale green or deep burgundy with initials monogrammed on the pockets. Maybe this was because Reilly had always slept in a T-shirt, usually with some silly saying printed on it. In fact, he did everything in a T-shirt to cover the beer-drinker's paunch beginning to show on his otherwise athletic body. She had to stop comparing every man she met to her ex-husband! Not all men had a concealed second personality, and she wasn't an easily dazzled seventeen-year-old anymore.

"They serve breakfast at the meeting. In the ball-room. At nine," she overexplained.

"I know, but I could meet you at the restaurant in your hotel. You can have your morning coffee while I have breakfast."

"Tea."

"What?"

"I'll have tea."

"Fine. Is eight o'clock too soon?" She could almost see his smile.

"I'll meet you there."

"Eight, then. And Brenda, I can't think of a nicer way to start the day."

Dropping the receiver back in place with a loud thunk, she ran her fingers through her hair and sank back on the pillow, but there was no way she was going back to sleep. Eric was going to ask her about the tour again, and her answer was no, emphatically no. Imagine spending three weeks with him, then saying good-bye!

One painful separation in her life was enough. If she ever fell in love again, it would be with someone who was her type: a quiet, stable man who liked home life and wanted kids. She didn't underestimate Eric's appeal, but she wasn't in the market for a fling with anyone.

For someone determined not to be seduced, she spent an inordinate amount of time deciding what to wear, finally narrowing it down to a choice between the gray suit she'd worn the day before and a navy pants suit that fit well but was a little prim. Ten minutes before she was supposed to meet him, she changed out of the gray outfit into the navy. After seeing her tailored image in the mirror, she wanted to change again, but if she did, there was a good chance she'd be late.

The first three elevators that stopped were loaded to capacity; on the fourth she was squeezed against a man gnawing on a pipe, forced to inhale fumes that smelled like a city dump while she worried about sparks burning her suit. The crush of bodies made the temperature in the car soar, and she was further discomforted by the realization that she was already eight minutes late.

Eric was reading a newspaper near the windowed entrance to a restaurant that was supposed to suggest Old New Orleans. He didn't look up until she spoke to him.

"Good morning," she said, noticing how relaxed and rested he looked; she'd tossed and turned all night.

"Hi."

He folded the newspaper and tucked it under his arm, gesturing for her to precede him. A broad-shouldered man greeted them with exuberant cheer, considering the time of day, and seated them at a table that seemed to be at the traffic hub of the whole restaurant. The breakfast rush was on, and it was sit there or go somewhere else, which she didn't have time to do.

Why was she reading the menu? She certainly didn't

want two breakfasts. A waiter came with a pot of coffee, filling Eric's cup with steaming liquid after she declined. Eric studied the menu, commenting that he wasn't a big breakfast eater. They were starting out just as they had last evening, distant and polite, strangers with not much to say to each other. Why had she been so eager to see him?

He urged her to join him in eating, then ordered a large orange juice and a bagel with cream cheese for himself. She still insisted all she wanted was tea.

"Are you a morning person or an evening person?" he asked, watching her pull the tea bag out of the little metal pot so the beverage wouldn't get too strong.

"Evening, I suppose. I like to stay up late, but I do my best work in the morning."

She didn't want to admit she was addicted to scary late-night movies, sometimes watching an old flick from the thirties until the wee hours. There were days when her working morning didn't begin until nearly noon.

"I watched an old horror movie until two A.M. last night," he admitted a little sheepishly.

"Which one?"

Dracula. The original."

"I love it! He just stares at his victims and you know he's reeking with evil. I must've seen it a dozen times."

"But have you seen *Dracula's Daughter?*" he teased.

"I've even seen *Dracula's Dog,* but nothing made in the seventies can compare with the oldies."

"My favorite is *Frankenstein.*"

"The 1931 version with Boris Karloff?"

"Of course!" He laughed with pleasure. "Next you'll be telling me you'd stay up all night to catch Lugosi and Chaney in *The Wolf Man* on 'The Late Late Show.'"

"Till dawn if necessary. The oldies play havoc with my writing schedule!"

Once the ice was broken, they talked and laughed like

old friends. She didn't remember her breakfast meeting until minutes before it was supposed to start.

"Play hookey," he urged when she told him she had to run.

She was tempted, but if she planned to write the conference off as a business expense, she should at least attend the meetings.

Eric was standing, waiting to slide back her chair, lightly touching her arm. If he asked again, she wouldn't be able to say no. He didn't.

He walked up the stairs to the lobby level with her, then left, promising to call her. He hadn't mentioned the tour again, and she wondered if her prim navy-blue pants suit had made him realize she wasn't the kind of woman he wanted as a traveling companion. Had he given up after last night's refusal, or had he decided his spur-of-the-moment idea wasn't such a good one? Maybe he'd changed his mind because escorting her from store to store wasn't worth three weeks of his time. Possibly he wasn't even interested in her as a woman. She'd never intended to go, but she still felt let down as she entered the ballroom where waiters were beginning to serve breakfast.

The choice of seating was practically nil; everyone at the conference seemed as determined as she was not to miss a moment. While she stood at the back trying to spot an empty chair, a young woman with glossy black curls handed her a white scarf with a heart motif printed in warm lavender. She absentmindedly knotted it around her neck before realizing it was a gift from a competing publisher. Would a Yankee wear a White Sox cap? She unknotted it with difficulty and folded it neatly; her mother would love it. Finally spotting a vacant chair, she asked if it was taken and was invited to join the eight other people at the table, all but one a woman. The lone man in a western-style shirt and string tie hardly spoke throughout the meal and disappeared immediately afterward, although some of the husbands and other men scattered around the room seemed to be enjoying themselves.

Brenda was soon so busy talking and listening, she forgot to eat most of her scrambled eggs and buttery croissant. On her right was a published historical writer, a young mother of two who'd come to the conference with her own mother. They traded stories about the difficulty of writing and selling, having suffered many of the same aggravations before being published. Brenda learned that the advances were usually larger for historical novels, but this writer averaged only one a year. Brenda had done as many as five, and her goal was six, a number many contemporary romance writers managed regularly. If she had a worry at this point in her career, it was that she'd burn out, reach a period when she just didn't have another romantic story in her. Maybe by then scary little horror stories would be back in the limelight.

The woman on her other side managed a bookshop in Arkansas and loved romances so much she'd just had to come to the conference. Brenda learned more from her than she did from the historical writer; the bookseller was an encyclopedia of information, sharing her frontline experiences with readers in a witty way. With supporters like her pushing romances, they'd still be selling like mad twenty years from now.

For the morning program, the glamorous award-winning artist Brenda had noticed the day before showed slides of all her romance covers, explaining how she rented costumes, researched the eras, and recruited models for her historical scenes. She photographed the people in costume in a variety of poses, then worked from the best shot. The results were stunning: gowns with velvety folds that seemed to have a real nap; long, flowing hair like spun silk; and lovers intensely involved with each other. It was an inspiration to Brenda to make her own characters more vivid, even though she painted her pictures with words, not oils.

The day went fast, with a chance in the afternoon to hear her publisher's senior editor offer ideas on how to write an exciting romance. Even though the Sheffield award had confirmed that she was at the top of the contemporary ladder, she had no illusions about staying there without grueling hard work. Not only at this conference, but everywhere she went, she talked to aspiring writers who loved romances and were trying to write or sell one of their own. Somewhere out there was a manuscript that would put all the current favorites in the shade. Thinking about it made her a little paranoid. She could imagine an army of thousands, each person bursting with wonderful stories to tell. What gave her a sense of security wasn't her success with romance; it was her experience in a variety of fields. The self-confidence of would-be romance writers was awe-inspiring. She'd timidly submitted and sold hundreds of short pieces before even imagining she could write a book. When people asked how she'd succeeded as a writer, she was genuinely at a loss to answer. At twenty-nine she had fifteen years of dogged determination behind her, and she was still sure she needed to improve.

At 11:15 that evening she finally flopped down on her bed, needing time to relax and mull over everything she'd seen and heard during the day, but all she thought about was Eric. Would he call her again? Why had he dropped the idea of a tour without saying a word to her? Did he regret his hasty invitation, using silence as a way to spare her feelings?

The trip to the conference was beginning to seem like a depressing mistake. Meeting a man like Eric made her feel dissatisfied with her life without offering any alternatives. She was fond of her friends at home, but her life would seem excruciatingly dull to him. Sometimes it was: being a single woman in a town where all her friends were married wasn't any picnic. Sometimes she felt like the odd one, the only one in her group who hadn't had children or made a success of marriage. Worse, some of her friends openly envied her success, not understanding that she still had to fill sixteen or so hours of her time every day, and an awful lot of it was spent alone. Her job didn't provide her with the circle of co-workers most people had, and regular outings with friends from her high school class weren't enough to completely dispel her bouts of loneliness.

Fighting off this brief flash of melancholy, she felt a stab of guilt for not being more grateful for all she'd accomplished. The conference was fun, and meeting Eric didn't change that. It hurt to think she might never see him again, but it was cruel of him to pretend more interest than he felt. It occurred to her for the first time that men could be terrible teases. Sometimes her understanding of the other half of the human race appalled her. She should be writing nursery tales instead of trying to plot stories about complicated male-female relationships! Once she'd read that psychologists went into their field to unravel the mysteries of their own minds. Maybe she was writing romances to work out some kind of understanding of men.

"Don't be ridiculous!" she said aloud, startling herself with the vehement statement. Sometimes she talked to Shakespeare, her noisy little parakeet, now vacationing on her neighbor's sun porch, but talking to herself was something new. "It's time to go home to Charlotte," she said, putting the emphasis on "-lotte" as only the natives did.

The phone was ringing, and remembering how Eric's call had roused her from sleep only that morning made her desperately want to hear his voice again. Just on the long shot, thousand-to-one chance that it was him, she let it ring several times before reaching for it with a distressingly unsteady hand.

"Brenda, thank heavens you're back!" Madge sounded harried and out of breath. "Do you know how many times I've tried to call you today? If I were feeding a pay phone, I would've blown a mink stole."

"What's the matter?" She had visions of canceled contracts, lawsuits over one of her books, or an angry publisher refusing to pay her royalties.

"It's not what's wrong. It's what's right."

Please, no riddles, Brenda wanted to beg. "Tell me!"

"Are you ready for this? You'd better sit. I have the opportunity of a lifetime for you."

"Not a book for Heartstring?" she asked without enthusiasm, wondering if her agent thought she was a writing machine capable of turning out copy as fast as she could type.

"No, no, no. I told you Learner didn't have much to offer. This is going to boost your sales like magic. It's a publicist's dream."

"Madge, will you please tell me!"

"Pack your bags! You're leaving on a three-week tour that will make *Passion's Pawn* a runaway best seller!"

"Oh, no!"

Now she knew why Eric hadn't said another word about visiting his stores. He'd gone to her agent instead.

"Oh, yes! Eric Sheffield is personally escorting you on a tour of his major stores from here to the Midwest. Philadelphia, Pittsburgh, Cleveland. Oh, I can't even remember all the stops. A whole slew of autograph parties and interviews. You won't believe how much he's spending on advertising alone. And the whole trip's at his expense."

"No way, Madge!"

"What?"

"I'm not going."

"Why on earth not?" Madge sounded stunned.

"For one thing, the conference isn't over. I don't want to miss the banquet tomorrow night."

"Brenda, I didn't say you're leaving tonight! You have to have your hair done, get some clothes, have a real make-over to wow your fans."

"I have three books to write."

"You could write six in the time you have!"

"Did you by any chance discuss travel arrangements?"

"A car. It's the only practical way to hit twenty-eight stores in twenty days."

"With Eric driving. It just won't work, Madge."

"You're serious about not wanting to go, aren't you?"

"Yes, I am. Eric asked me yesterday if I'd go. I said no. How do you think I feel, having him go to you after I refused?"

"I can see why you're irritated—but, Brenda, think! You've got to consider what an opportunity this is for you."

"Spending three weeks with Eric? I don't for a minute believe it's my career he's interested in."

"Has he been coming on to you?" Madge sounded worried.

"Not exactly. We had dinner."

"He must have done something to make you so hostile," the agent said in her most practical tone. "Did he invite you up to his room? Try to seduce you? Get fresh? Make innuendos?"

"None of those," Brenda admitted, "but he said the tour was a spur-of-the-moment idea to spend three weeks with me."

"Look, I'll get him on the phone and lay down some

stipulations—separate rooms, a guaranteed businesslike arrangement . . ."

"No!"

Even the thought of Madge telling him he'd have to be a good boy embarrassed her. She wasn't a baby! Did her agent think she was acting like one?

"Trust me, Brenda. You really should go. He's already placed rush orders for thousands of extra copies of *Passion's Pawn* and talked to your publisher about a new display idea he has for the whole line. A photographer is going to take some stills of you for Valjean so she can paint a life-size mock-up. You'll be able to meet a cardboard copy of yourself in Sheffield stores all over the country. I think Eric's paying for most of that too."

Brenda felt trapped. If she refused to go now, she'd look like an idiot.

"The competition is fierce in the romance lines now. Writers would kill for a chance like this," Madge went on, not really believing her client would walk away from such a great campaign. "Oh, and jot down your measurements—height, bust, waist, hips, just the standard ones. Give them to the photographer, and he'll pass them on to the artist."

"I haven't said I'd go!"

The awful thing was, Madge knew she was doing a wonderful thing for her client by urging her to go. Reasonably speaking, she was, but Brenda still seethed, so upset with Eric for springing this trap that she didn't care if she never saw him again.

"It's your decision," Madge said, not trying to hide her acute disappointment, "but I have seven other romance writers who'd do anything for an opportunity like this."

"The question is, What am I supposed to do to earn it?" Brenda asked so softly her agent asked her to repeat it. She did.

62

"Nothing! Just sell books for Sheffield. Oh, and I talked to your editor. She's wildly enthusiastic. The whole publishing house is behind you on this."

"What if I do a lousy job?"

"You won't. You've been to autograph parties before. Just smile, sign your name, and answer questions. It'll get tiring, but remember, everyone who buys a book has friends, sisters, mothers, cousins, acquaintances. People love to have an autographed novel on their coffee tables, and they're much less apt to loan it or take it to a paperback exchange."

Everything Madge said made good sense; Brenda knew she'd look foolish if she refused. Eric had used heavy clout to bypass her objections; when he talked about persuasion, he meant intimidation. She'd never forgive him for using her publisher and agent to corner her into going. He'd remember this trip for a long, long time, but not for the reasons he anticipated.

"I guess I'm going on tour."

"You won't regret it."

After more encouragement and instructions from Madge, she let the receiver fall back into place. The Yellow Pages of the Manhattan phone directory were clamped between hard covers, too thick and heavy to balance on her knees so she bounced the book on the bed, parting the pages at the HOTELS section. For a minute she couldn't remember the name of Eric's hotel, and when she did, it seemed to take ages to find the number. Not until she'd jotted it on a note pad from her purse did she notice the hotel's big ad with the numbers half an inch high.

Seventy-five cents for local calls, she noted with annoyance, wondering why they didn't charge to walk on the sidewalks in New York. The instructions for getting an outside line were buried in a sheath of instructions as complicated as the guidelines for assembling a computer, and she impatiently took a shortcut and rang the operator, finally getting the right switchboard to ring Eric's room.

"Yes." The muffled voice didn't sound like his.

"Eric?"

"Yes."

Of course, he was sleeping peacefully. He knew his plan was foolproof.

"Why didn't you tell me?"

"Brenda?"

"Yes, Brenda!"

"Let me wake up a minute."

She wasn't going to give him time to invent an excuse.

"You could've had the courtesy to tell me you were contacting my agent and editor and publisher."

He also could have spared her the unhappiness of thinking he'd changed his mind.

"Why do you have an agent if you don't want her to help you?"

A good question: Why did she need an agent who meddled in her personal life? Brenda was still angry, but not too furious to know she was being unfair to Madge.

"You could've talked to me about it!"

"Sweetheart, I did." His teasing tone added fuel to her anger; he sounded like a man who'd just pulled off a good joke.

"But you didn't have to pressure me like that!"

"Did your agent fill you in on all the details? We have some things to do before we leave. I'll pick you up outside your hotel Monday morning at nine."

"You really expect me to be there?"

"Isn't your agent authorized to make commitments for you? I haven't heard to the contrary from her."

She hated his self-assurance, his casual assumption

64

that she'd fall in with his plans. Too angry to say more, she was ready to hang up when he chuckled softly.

"It won't be so bad. You'll see. Give it half a chance, and you might have a good time."

"Neither of us will," she predicted bleakly, breaking off their conversation without saying good-bye.

The next person to use the Yellow Pages would wonder why a ballpoint pen had been jabbed into the hotel section.

CHAPTER FOUR

The giant red balloon in her hand pulled her above the mist until she was floating in a cobalt-blue sky studded with cumulus clouds: a snowy unicorn, an elf, and fanciful mountains of fluff. Ahead the sun reflected off the silvery suit of a distant knight, his visor down and his lance held in a gloved hand. They bounded toward each other, their love giving them longer strides than seven-league boots until, with sudden panic, Brenda saw great danger ahead. She tried to warn her armored lover, but her cry was too late! His lance point punctured her balloon, and she tumbled, tumbled, tumbled. . . .

She awoke with a start, sure for a moment that she'd cried aloud a warning to her fantasy knight. It took a few seconds to remember where she was and why her sleep had been so dream-filled and restless. It was Monday, the day she'd planned to go home. The excitement of the convention and the thrill of having a fascinating man show interest in her were gone; in their place she had a sour taste and a guilty reluctance to get up and face the day. She was being given a marvelous career opportunity but she couldn't summon any enthusiasm. Why hadn't Eric persuaded her to go instead of working behind her back? Neither her dread of public appearances nor her wariness about getting seriously involved with him would have stood up under the full impact of his charm, she admitted to herself now. But how could he be so high-handed, arranging the whole trip with her agent and publisher, then cornering her into going? He was so unfair! He'd outmaneuvered her instead of trying to involve her in his planning. Did he always resort to crafty means when his first attempt failed?

She could still refuse to go. Crawling lethargically out of bed, she toyed with the idea of canceling the tour and making a beeline for the airport, even if it meant sitting there all day waiting for a flight to Chicago on standby. By the time she'd finished her shower, this still seemed like the best way out, but she didn't have enough nerve to take the cowardly course. Unfortunately she'd always cared what others thought of her, and she didn't want to look like a fool to her agent and publisher. There wasn't one good, logical reason not to take advantage of Eric's great promotional tour.

Some of the things Madge had told her were just beginning to sink in. Imagine meeting a life-size paper doll of herself in a bookstore!

She couldn't stand all day, staring moodily out the window, watching the city come alive on the pavement below. Eric had already seen her severe navy pants suit, but she wore it anyway, buttoning a pink oxford-cloth blouse to her throat.

She had to let two crowded elevators go by without her before one stopped with standing room. According to her watch, Eric had already been parked outside for several minutes. He'd think she was deliberately late. He deserved to wait, but she hadn't intended this petty revenge.

Eric was coming into the lobby as she was walking out.

"How long do you think the doorman can keep my car from being towed away?" he asked.

She refused to apologize, and there wasn't much else to say.

How much did he tip the doorman who let him use the precious length of curb space? Brenda couldn't see the bill that changed hands, but she felt depressed by her plebeian attitude. Her whole life was being turned topsy-turvy, and she was still trying to unravel the protocol of the big-city system of gratuities. It didn't console her to know that she'd probably use that detail in a book someday.

"Are you going to get into the car?" Eric asked.

The doorman shot her a questioning look. Did he think she expected him to open the car door for her? She quickly seated herself inside the dark green car before he could perform that service; at least she avoided another decision about tipping.

"Do I really have a choice?" she asked Eric, banging the door harder than she'd intended.

"I'm not abducting you."

Where was the charm that brought cheers at the convention?

"No, but you've put me in a position where I'll look silly if I don't go."

"That wasn't my intention. I thought this trip would be good for your career and my business—a boon for both of us."

"Both of us?" She didn't try to hide her skepticism.

"My customers like the excitement of author visits, and they give the store managers more incentive to promote. After they meet you, you'll be more than just another name on a cover."

Beside them a taxi squealed its brakes at the light,

and a wave of pedestrians swept in front of the car. The signal switched to DON'T WALK, but the stream of people kept coming. When the light changed to green, the cab driver went forward, seemingly heedless of the stragglers still trying to cross. Eric waited for a stout woman in chartreuse slacks to move out of his path, not threatening her with his bumper like the typical city driver. Brenda liked him for that, at least.

"I'm going to drop you off at the salon and take care of some business of my own while you're there."

She was much more interested in seeing more of Manhattan than she was in her destination. Madge had said something about a "make-over" before her appointment with the photographer, but she'd been too upset to ask what a "make-over" entailed. Now she'd much rather do more sightseeing. There wasn't an inch of the city that she didn't want to see before going back to her quiet little hometown, although she'd never felt any burning desire to relocate in a metropolis. People were space-poor in big cities; the great brick blocks of low-cost housing at the tip of the island reminded her of an unfenced prison. It didn't seem natural for people to live like bees in a hive, stacked up in little cells.

"This is the car you're driving on the tour?" she asked when the silence between them became uncomfortable.

"That's why I rented it."

More aware of him than she wanted to be, she kept her eyes riveted on the city outside the passenger window, but she couldn't shut off her other senses. The scent of his after-shave was mildly erotic, making her wonder how it would feel to rub her cheek against his. He hummed softly under his breath, a low, unmelodic rendition of an unidentifiable tune repeated over and over until she suspected it was done to annoy her. Just when she was going to ask him to stop, he swerved out of the flow of traffic and pulled up to a curb.

"You put up with my humming longer than most people," he said cheerfully. "You have an appointment with Andre." She stepped out of the car and as she shut the door, he yelled, "I'll come back here for you in three hours or so."

Three hours! He'd driven away before she had a chance to challenge him. How could it possibly take three hours to restyle her hair?

The salon was impressively large, with gold flocked wallpaper, gilt mirrors, and discreet cubbyholes for customer privacy. If they asked her to take off her clothes, she was leaving. No way would she lie around for hours in avocado slime, tour or no tour!

A slender young man with curly black hair and long eyelashes ushered her into a curtained area, introducing himself as Andre.

"Just lie back and relax," he crooned, seating her in a burgundy chair that matched his uniform and tilted back like a dentist's.

"I'd rather keep my hair fairly long," she started to explain, not at all sure she liked the way he was dismantling her bun, loosely fingering, then cutting off, a single hair.

He carried the hair to a device on the counter, mumbling over it and apparently getting some kind of reading when he inserted it into the machine.

"Computer readouts for hair?" she joked.

"Something like that." He smiled mysteriously. "Your hair's in very good condition, considering."

She didn't ask what he meant by "considering."

Andre was only captain of the team. He sent her to the shampooer, then supervised the plucking of her brows, gave directions for her facial and manicure, and cut and styled her hair himself, completely ignoring her gasps of protest when alarmingly long strands of hair went flying to the floor.

"You'll love this," he repeated at thirty-second intervals, clicking his teeth in rhythm with his shears.

After magnanimously deciding she didn't need a permanent, he gave her detailed instructions and a demonstration on using a curling iron to keep the sleek, shoulder-length waves the way he wanted them. Not surprisingly, he included the curling iron in the take-home beauty kit he was assembling for her.

The makeup session she enjoyed. Her operator was young but skillful, applying a heavenly shade of violet eye shadow Brenda never would have thought of using herself.

"Beautiful," Andre said with a great deal of self-satisfaction when he came back to assess the results of his labor.

There was nothing so crass as a cash register in sight, and Brenda wasn't at all sure how the "patrons" paid their "consultants." She opened her purse with a tentative gesture, hoping for some instructions from her consultant, Andre. What on earth should she do about tipping? Would an artist like Andre be insulted if she handed him a bill? Or if she didn't? She fumbled with her billfold, still hoping for inspired guidance.

"No, no, Brenda."

If Onassis came into the salon, would she be called Jackie?

"You've done a marvelous job, so . . ." She kept her hand in her purse.

"Mr. Sheffield has taken care of everything," he assured her with a regal gesture of dismissal.

"Andre, you're a genius!" Brenda and the beauty consultant turned to see Eric striding toward them flashing a victorious smile. He extended his hand and shook Andre's vigorously. "Honestly, Andre, I didn't

71

even recognize her! You've done an outstanding job. She looks beautiful!" His eyes studied her silky ebony-colored hair, the hint of violet shadow around her blue-gray eyes, and her full, wine-colored lips. *She looks just like one of her heroines,* he said to himself. Too self-conscious to give vent to her anger, Brenda tried not to blush under Eric's scrutiny. When his gaze dropped from her face to her body, she too looked down at her navy pants suit.

"My beautiful Brenda," Eric began, "we have one more stop to make." Before Brenda could protest, Eric grabbed her hand and swept her out of the salon and hurried her into a clothing boutique a few doors away.

"I don't need clothes," she insisted.

"Think of them as costumes. You have to sell yourself to sell books. People who see you in this red dress will remember you." He added it to the pile he wanted her to try on.

"My grandmother will have a stroke if she sees me in this."

Eric was hovering by the entrance to the dressing rooms, passing judgment on every outfit she reluctantly modeled for him. His exuberance was wearing on her nerves, making her decidedly grumpy.

"I pay for my own clothes," she insisted, handing the saleswoman a piece of plastic that no business ever refused.

"I'm sorry, miss. We don't accept credit cards."

"Everyone accepts this one," Brenda insisted.

"I'm so sorry."

The saleswoman did, however, accept Eric's check.

"You arranged that," she accused him as they left the boutique with an awkward number of packages.

"Just a business expense," he assured her.

The studio was a stark white room strewn with cameras, cables, lights, and screens, and the photographer

72

was a twin of the obnoxious balloon man at the conference. He called her darling but hissed when he said it. The lights gave her a headache, but the man behind the camera was a much bigger pain. At Eric's suggestion, she wore the filmy red dress, trying to smile as the cameraman snapped her standing and sitting, leaning and reclining, limp and tense. Eric stayed in a shadowy corner of the room, occasionally giving whispered suggestions to the photographer. She'd never felt more like an inanimate object.

Someone ate dinner that evening with Eric Sheffield, slept fitfully in a bed at the Roosevelt, and awoke early to pack luggage and check out, but Brenda wasn't at all sure it was her. The face that stared back from the mirror after she curled her hair and put on her makeup vaguely resembled the old Brenda, but was more like a new, glamorous stranger. What was a scribbler, a daydreamer, a teller of stories doing masquerading as a vamp, a siren? What was Brenda Storm doing getting ready to leave on a cross-country jaunt with a man who could turn her knees to gelatin with a smile?

She was ready on time and their departure went off like clockwork. In fact, that was how she felt: like one of the figures on an ancient clock, emerging when the hour struck.

They rode for quite a while before she allowed herself the luxury of a quick glance at his profile. He was more handsome from the side than the front. The regularity of his features had made her think he was ordinary-looking from the back of the ballroom, but in profile his lean chin line, smoothly chiseled nose, high cheekbones, and even forehead were a sculptor's ideal. She bit her lip and stared moodily at a purple florist's van passing them on the right. Eric was driving slowly in a fast lane. This was going to be the longest trip of her life.

Trying not to look in his direction again made her

neck feel stiff and her eyelids heavy. To give herself a moment of respite, she lay back against the headrest and closed her eyes, forgetting how poorly she'd slept the night before.

"Brenda."

A feathery kiss on the corner of her mouth tickled and roused her to instant wakefulness.

"Our first stop," Eric explained, his smile teasing her.

"Where are we?"

"Near King of Prussia."

"I thought we were going to Philadelphia."

"We're northwest of it. I don't have a store in the inner city."

"I don't believe I slept so long."

"You did. Soundly."

The skirt of a new deep rose suit had ridden above her knees, and she wondered again if such a vibrant color was her style. She tugged on the skirt before getting out of the car, a gesture he certainly didn't miss.

"I'd like to wake up and be in Charlotte," she said irritably to cover the agitation she felt.

"Wait a minute." He caught her arm in a strong grasp.

"Please let go."

He did, but his steady gaze held her more firmly than his hand. "Can we be amiable about this?"

"I didn't realize we weren't."

He raised his brows in doubt. "I can tell you're unhappy."

"I like to handle my own affairs." She immediately knew that was a bad way to phrase it.

"So do I. We're talking about your career. How many autograph parties have you had for *Passion's Pawn?*"

"None."

"TV appearances?"

She shook her head.

74

"Newspaper releases? Speaking engagements?"

"I write books. My publisher does the selling."

"Wrong! You have to look out for your own interests. How many books come out of the house every year? And how much of their budget goes into promoting your book?"

"I have no idea, but my books did well last year. I try to tell the best possible story and . . ."

"You can't sit on your rear and expect this year and the next and the one after next to be great ones."

"Who appointed you my publicist?" she snapped, again reaching for the door handle.

"I just want you to realize that publicity is essential to keep your career rolling."

"I'm here. Isn't that enough?"

"Not nearly enough!" he said grimly, ignoring the curious stares of the family emerging from a van parked next to his rented Oldsmobile.

For a wild instant she wasn't sure whether he wanted to kiss her or sock her, then composure washed over him like a cooling breeze.

"Just try to be a little more congenial with your fans," he said gruffly.

She was still upset when she saw the entrance to Shef-field's Bookshelf. A large pink poster with flaming red letters announced that Brenda Storm would be there today to autograph her books. Copies of three of her books were stacked and spread out on a table set off by a low centerpiece of pink rosebuds and carnations. It was lovely, really, but it meant she'd sit facing the mall traffic, squirming with embarrassment when people stared at her like a caged monkey. She was absolutely sure no one would buy a book, and if they did, what should she write? A simple signature seemed too stingy, and she wasn't clever about little sayings. Her sister always bought cards without messages for birthdays and holidays, writing her own highly personal, beautifully appropriate words. Brenda the Writer never came up with anything more original than "Get well soon" or "Have a nice birthday."

She didn't have much time to muse over the vagaries of talent. Eric ushered her into the store and was met by a striking blonde in her mid-thirties. Just his age, Brenda noted with displeasure, wondering what to do with her purse. Should she plunk it down any old place and risk having it snatched if she got busy, or keep it clutched between her feet, the strap secured under one heel?

"Mr. Sheffield, it's such a pleasure to see you!" the woman said enthusiastically.

She had a beautiful nose, patrician and straight; no one would ever mistake her for a Barbie Doll.

"I'd like you to meet Brenda Storm," Eric was saying.

Brenda dutifully offered her hand, wondering what he'd said about her that she'd missed. The store manager greeted her almost as cordially as she had the head of the company. Almost. Brenda found herself seated at the table with a flurry of compliments, then the manager lured Eric to her office in the back room.

Good grief, Brenda thought with panic, she'd be there for two hours, and she hadn't even thought to make a quick trip to the restroom. Her hairstyle had to be crushed after sleeping all the way from New York, and she hadn't had a chance to look in a mirror to see if her eye shadow or lipstick was smudged. Somehow she'd expected to use the bookstore lounge to freshen up.

Her first reader brought a book she'd purchased somewhere else a few days ago, but Brenda was so grateful she wanted to hug her. She kept the woman beside the table as long as possible talking about books, kids, and even the weather.

A harried-looking young woman with a baby in a stroller and a toddler trying to pull away from her hand stopped and asked how much money romance writers made. Brenda told her, honestly enough, that it varied greatly depending on the publisher and the writer, but the woman was insistent, wanting an exact figure, and looked cross when Brenda said she hadn't received a royalty check yet that spring. The toddler slid to his bottom and started screaming, and the mother left without buying a book. How could she possibly find time to read, let alone write? Brenda supposed she would always make time to write, but she was mildly envious of the young mother, adoring the two red-cheeked tots and wishing that someday she'd have at least one child of her own.

Another young woman, who said she worked at the jewelry store across the way, asked which book Brenda thought was her best. Brenda's honest answer seemed to confuse her: her sister liked *Lingering Love,* her editor seemed to favor *Passion's Pawn,* but she was partial to *Hasty Desire.* Brushing a strawberry-blond curl away from her forehead, the woman promised to buy one of them on payday.

I'm doing more harm than good, Brenda thought, wanting a glass of cold water more than she wanted to sell the whole display of books. Undoubtedly she could have one if she asked, but she felt like an elementary school student told not to leave her desk.

Her day took a turn for the better when a genuine romance enthusiast stopped to talk about her favorite kind of book, buying all three to be autographed even though she already had one of them. The romance fan's good spirits and appreciation carried Brenda through the next hour, which consisted mostly of watching shoppers stroll by and read the sign. A few seemed embarrassed to pass without stopping, averting their eyes when Brenda looked at them.

Was Eric auditing the store's accounts, taking inventory in the back room? Or was he making an inventory of the manager's assets? Surprised at how much she resented his absence, she shifted restlessly on the hard chair, welcoming a chat with one of the bookstore's clerks, who came over to introduce himself. He had a master's degree in psychology but seemed to have found a semipermanent niche in the book business. He wanted to talk about rape fantasies and masochism in romance novels. Brenda sent him off to get her a glass of water instead, deciding there was no point in challenging him to find either in her books. She wasn't very patient with critics who didn't bother to read romances before knocking them.

A sweet white-haired old lady stopped to apologize for buying all of Brenda's books at a used-book exchange; it was the only way she could afford them on social security, she explained. Her companion, steelhaired but younger, reproved her for reading such nonsense.

Brenda wondered again what Eric was doing in back with the manager. She'd expected him to meet the customers with her, turning on his charm for romance readers, making the tour a team effort of writer and bookseller.

A short, hesitant woman with tight dark curls who was carrying two romance novels by another author warily circled the table, afraid to actually commit herself by picking up a book.

"What are your books about?" she asked curiously.

"The copy on the back covers probably describes them better than I can," Brenda answered politely. "Why don't you read them?"

The woman leaned forward, keeping the maximum distance between herself and the table, and plucked a book from one of the piles. She slowly read the back of *Passion's Pawn*, then opened the cover and seriously studied the excerpt in the front. After repeating the procedure for all three books, she replaced them and walked away. Brenda sighed audibly, wondering again whether it did more harm than good to let readers see the author. Eight long minutes later the same woman returned with only one rival romance in hand and took a copy of *Passion's Pawn*.

"If I like it, I'll buy the others too."

Wanting to quit after this triumph, Brenda again looked at her watch and was nearly drenched by the glass of water the bookstore psychologist was handing her. Fortunately a lineup at the cash register forced him to abandon another attempt to discuss the psychological undercurrents in her novels.

The water churned in her totally empty stomach. She'd skipped breakfast, and Eric had yet to mention a lunch break.

"How's it going?" he asked cheerfully, finally making an appearance with the blond store manager at his elbow.

"Four books sold," she said wryly. "Three of them to one person."

She wanted to point out that her royalties for this signing party averaged out to an hourly wage of thirty-two cents. For this she had lost her identity, let a man buy clothes for her, and tried to cope with a gnawing case of stage fright.

"I am so sorry there wasn't time to run an ad in the newspaper," the manager said, her tone faultlessly apologetic.

"I'll be back in about twenty minutes when your time

is up," Eric told Brenda. "I'll get you a sandwich, so we can leave right away for the next store."

He touched the manager's arm, and they walked into the mall together, disappearing out of sight around the corner of a candy store. Brenda stood and watched them, not at all embarrassed to be observing them. They were undoubtedly going for lunch. If hers was much later, she'd faint. She didn't drink the rest of the water, staring dejectedly as the glass made a wet circle on the blond formica tabletop. Maybe her next heroine would have raven-black hair; she was thoroughly sick of blondes.

A delightfully pleasant fan bought the last book she sold, stopping to chat about how much she enjoyed romances. Brenda was so grateful she took the woman's name and address, promising to send her a card when the next book was scheduled.

Her time was up, so she left, seeking out a restroom to freshen up, then dashing into a sandwich bar for a tuna salad and a carton of milk to go, too hungry to gamble on Eric remembering to bring her something. He was nowhere in sight when she got back to the bookstore. She sat at the table, feeling awkward now that the time printed on the poster for her appearance was over, wishing she had enough nerve to eat her sandwich right there.

When Eric did return with the manager, he was carrying a small paper bag with bright red and yellow stripes.

"I hope you like pastrami and cola," he said, handing it to her.

"Tuna and milk," she said, glad to show him she wouldn't starve while he dawdled with his employee. "I wasn't sure you'd remember."

The next store was busier and more fun, since the manager was an avid romance reader herself who'd personally invited many of her friends and customers. Brenda didn't know if the woman had called in all the people who owed her favors or if she had a huge supply of relatives, but the welcoming crowd kept her busy talking and signing books beyond the advertised time. Eric spent most of his time in this store hovering over the table and exercising his charm on the customers. The manager was over fifty and not at all awed by the company president. Brenda adored her.

"I made motel reservations in Lancaster," he said. "I thought it'd be better to drive an hour or so now and start fresh at the store there in the morning."

She studied the stain on the little writer's bump on her longest finger, refusing to show any interest in his plans. If they included any more managers like the blonde at the first store, she'd better start carrying a lunch.

CHAPTER FIVE

Their day ended with a leisurely Italian dinner, spicy spaghetti and ribs, and for the second night in a row Brenda retired early to her motel room, declining Eric's offer to see what entertainment the town might provide. She could refuse to spend the evening with him, but she couldn't suppress her curiosity about what he was doing. Her ears tingled with alertness, straining for sounds from the room next to hers. For a motel decorated with prosaic green carpeting, gold spreads, and dime-store art reproductions, the soundproofing was top-notch. The few faint noises that penetrated her room were too muffled to distinguish.

Could she go on with this for three weeks? The first store had been the worst, but traveling with Eric was draining her. When he smiled, she wanted to please him, but she felt more and more like a traveling freak show, put on display by the charming Mr. Sheffield. Whatever she'd expected, it wasn't this impersonal business relationship. She could almost feel him keeping her at arm's length in spite of his polite invitations to join him in the evenings.

And you were afraid he'd try to seduce you! she

taunted herself, tossing aside the large white towel from her shower and glancing at her naked image from head to thighs in the dresser mirror. Her breasts were full and firm and her waist slender, but how many more rich Italian dinners could her figure tolerate? With her thirtieth birthday looming ahead, maybe it was time to remarry. A nice comfortable man like her father could give her babies and a quiet home, never mind that she didn't shiver with excitement at the thought of any of the eligible men in Charlotte. The sensations Eric created just by looking into her eyes or touching her hand were illusions, snares to her common sense.

She ran her hands down her sides, spreading her fingers over her small waist and outlining her hips. Enough of that! She hastily slipped into a white cotton nightgown with eyelet straps and trim. It reached just to her knees, and she should have felt cool. The air outside was hovering in the low fifties, but inside this vacuum-sealed room with its immovable windows, she was cooking. On impulse she examined the room's heating and air-conditioning unit, pressing the button to send a gust of icy air into her face. Leaning over the blast, she let it billow under her gown until her flesh was all goosebumps.

"Better than a cold shower," she said aloud, clenching her teeth so they wouldn't chatter and dashing under the covers of the bed.

She didn't turn off the air. The manager would hate her for squandering energy but she couldn't explain to him that she was traveling with a man who inflamed her.

She'd never felt less sleepy, and cold skin didn't really extinguish the source of her feverish warmth. But no matter what it cost her, she'd show Eric that she didn't appreciate his high-handed tactics in arranging the tour.

So far she hadn't had the satisfaction of refusing him; he was behaving like a scoutmaster, not a lecherous rake.

A firm knock made her bound to the tiny security viewer set in the door. She shouldn't have been surprised to see Eric. Who else did she know at this motel? But nonetheless she hadn't expected him to pay her a nighttime visit.

She swore she'd never travel without a robe again! Making a quick circuit of the room, she turned off the air conditioner and grabbed her coat from the open rack, trying to ignore his repeated knocking while she buttoned it.

"I thought you'd gone out," he said. "Do you sleep in your raincoat?"

"Of course not. I didn't bring a robe."

"It's freezing in here. Let me see if your heat is working."

"No! I mean, I like to sleep in a cool room."

He lightly touched one of her hands and whistled. "Your fingers are like ice."

Bending over the temperature control unit in the far corner, he felt the cold metal grillwork and turned a puzzled face toward her. "You've been running the air conditioner?"

"I felt a little warm."

"Oh?" He raised his brows, doubting her with a teasing expression.

"These rooms get stuffy."

"Mine doesn't seem to be."

"I thought you were going out."

"No, not unless you've changed your mind about coming with me."

"I haven't."

She was still standing by the door, her hand on the knob to see him out.

"I don't want you catching cold," he said.

84

"You might have to cancel the tour."

"Have your autograph parties been so bad?"

"No, aside from the first one they've been pleasant," she admitted, hoping he remembered that the blond manager had hosted the poorly publicized one.

Someone else knocked on her door, and Eric moved forward to open it.

"Bring it right in."

A young waiter in a white shirt and bow tie pushed a cart past Brenda, positioning it for some reason of his own between the coat rack and the bathroom. Eric signed the bill, reached into his pocket for a tip, and ushered the motel employee out of the room. A bottle of champagne, the green glass damply misted below a gold foil-covered cork, rested in a silver bucket of ice with two stemmed goblets beside it.

This was the first time she'd seen him without a jacket, his shoulders flexing under the fine cotton of his shirt. For a moment she was fascinated by the stripes, white on white, differentiated by the sheen of the fabric. The sleeves were rolled to his elbows, and the hairs on his forearms were dark and fine, tempting her to stroke them with her fingertips.

"I really don't think . . ." she began defensively, wishing he'd turn into a troll with skin like a toad and bulging frog eyes so she could summon up enough resistance to throw him out.

"I'm not going to drink champagne with a woman in a raincoat," he said with a gentle smile that liquefied her legs.

She'd written the big champagne seduction scene at least three times, but now that it was happening to her, it was totally unreal. Did he really think she'd melt in his arms after a few glasses of bubbly wine?

Your heroines always do, she reminded herself, watching with trepidation as Eric slowly came closer.

His fingers lightly stroked her cheek, then traced the outline of her lips, one tip parting them and feeling the ivory-smooth surface of her teeth.

"No," she murmured weakly.

"Yes." His mouth covered hers, sucking the sweetness from her full lips until her breath felt trapped like a balloon in her chest. When he released her she was dizzy from more than lack of air.

He started with the top button, touching nothing but her coat, his head bent in concentration. The rich brown of his hair attracted her fingers, and she ran them over his scalp, promising herself she'd stop him when the last button was open. Sliding the coat off her shoulders, he discarded it on the bed and kneaded her shoulders, inching closer until she was in his arms, lifting her face to receive his kiss. This was what she'd expected, but it was much more, a gentle, persuasive assault on her senses that made her cling to his shoulders, limp with longing as he slowly and thoroughly kissed away her resistance. His lips were firm, making hers tingle, but they moved over her eyelids, her ears, the hollow of her throat, with the gentleness of dew on a rose petal.

"Just a business trip," she murmured, paralyzed by the trail of kisses on her throat.

"Is that what you want?"

His hands moved down her spine, caressing the small of her back and the curve of her hip, spreading his fingers across her bottom to press her closer.

"You're beautiful," he whispered, burying his face in the sleek mass of dark hair.

Beautiful now, she thought uncomfortably, remembering only too well that he had arranged to have her remade according to his own ideas. Could the real Brenda, hair in a bun and face free of makeup, stir him this way?

His hands found the hem of her gown, slipping under it to arouse her with intimate caresses while his mouth clung to hers, savoring the sweetness of her response. Skillful and merciless, he summoned from her the responses he wanted with expert confidence. When he parted her thighs to caress her there, she pushed his hand away. Embarrassed because she'd been stirred to such deep pleasure so quickly, she backed away.

"No, Eric."

Ignoring her protest, he sat on the edge of the bed, pulling her down on his lap and caressing her thigh. She stopped his hand only to feel the warmth of his breath against her throat.

"No." Her objections were growing weak as he slid one strap from her shoulder, exposing the top of her breast, teasing the pink tip until it hardened under his tongue.

"Why don't you unbutton my shirt?" he asked, kissing her again and guiding her hand to the edge of his beltless waistband.

Sliding a finger into an opening of his shirt, she slowly freed one button and then another, loving the firm warmth of his skin and the silkiness of the hair sprinkled on it, wanting to cushion her cheek on the protective expanse of his chest.

"Your heroine did wonderful things with her tongue in *Passion's Pawn*," he whispered, opening the rest of his buttons more quickly himself.

"I'm not my heroine!" She backed away so abruptly she nearly fell, feeling red heat rush to her face.

"What's wrong?" He stood and followed her, looking genuinely puzzled.

"I write fantasy! I'm not one of my heroines, I'm in no way like them!"

"I liked Gina in your book. See, I even remember her name."

"But she isn't me!"

"I haven't insulted you! She's lively and fun and sexy in a positive way."

"Just please leave, Eric."

"Tell me why."

"I want you to."

"You didn't a minute ago."

"I just didn't say so."

"I wasn't forcing myself on you." He held both hands in front of him, spreading the fingers, reminding her of how they felt caressing her back, kneading her sensitive buttocks, invading and persuading.

"Just go!" She couldn't look at him anymore.

"Brenda." He stood behind her, so close she could feel the warmth he radiated. "Just tell me why the sudden turnoff."

"I didn't want this trip, and I don't want to make love."

"You did a few minutes ago."

"That was a terrible mistake."

"You're making the terrible mistake," he said, exasperated.

"Please leave, Eric."

"Not until we talk."

"Not now." She still wouldn't look at him.

"Did your husband hurt you that badly?" His voice was low and compassionate, bringing tears of frustration to her eyes.

"He has nothing to do with this."

"No? Then tell me why you're warm and sweet one minute and cold and bitter the next?"

"That's only the way *you* see me."

"I think you're still mad about this trip, and that's crazy."

"You practically forced me to come."

"Hardly! Your agent thought you'd be dumb to refuse."

"It's not my agent you're trying to get to bed!"

"I knew that's what you thought when I first suggested it! That's why I didn't know how to persuade you."

"And of course, when you asked, you weren't planning a champagne love-in?"

"I wanted to get to know a beautiful, desirable woman. Are you condemning me for that?"

"I just want you to leave this room!"

"And waste a bottle of champagne?"

"Take it with you."

"I never drink alone."

"I don't care if you shampoo with it. Just get out!"

"I think," he said slowly, "that you're fighting yourself, not me."

"You're wrong!"

"Am I?"

When she moved, he moved, staying only inches away but not touching her.

"Look at me and tell me to go," he demanded. "Then I might believe you mean it."

"You came to drink champagne," she said with mock bravado, skirting around him and moving quickly to the cart between the beds.

Peeling off the foil, she struggled to remove the cork.

"Let me," he said.

"I'm not helpless!"

Without answering, he took the bottle from her, opening it with a popping sound that emphasized the silence between them. She replaced the strap of her nightgown that had slipped off her shoulder while he filled the two goblets to their rims.

"I can't think of an appropriate toast," he said, grin-

89

ning, handing a glass to her and drinking deeply himself.

Sitting on the bed, he slowly ran his eyes up her body from her navy satin mules to the silky brown hair that almost touched her shoulders.

"This isn't why I wanted you to tour," he said emphatically. "I hope you believe me."

"I don't know what to believe. There are hundreds of romance writers who'd love to do this. Why me?"

"You're the award winner. I told you, it's good for the bookstore business to have popular authors visit."

"So you only want me to boost your business?"

Confused and miserable, she didn't know if it was worse to be used to promote his business or to be desired as a woman he'd remodeled to his own specifications.

"Brenda, if I've offended you by wanting to make love to you, I'm sorry."

His apology made her feel warm, but she didn't understand why.

"I think I should go home now."

"No way. You're committed. I've made too many arrangements to cancel them now."

"You can easily cancel my appearances at your own stores."

"There's more to this than just going to the stores. The day after tomorrow my manager in Benedict, Ohio, has you booked for the dedication of a library wing. The program chairman was trying to round up some authors, so it's perfect for you." He stood up and began to pace, speaking in a low and businesslike voice. "You'll need a two- or three-minute speech about how important libraries are to your work." He swallowed champagne too quickly, coughed, and lost his composure for an instant, letting his anger show. "Just say you do all

90

the research for your books in libraries. I may be the only one listening who believes it."

"Is that another reason for this trip, to give me an opportunity to do some research?"

"Think what you like." He refilled her half-empty glass and his empty one. "But you'll need to wear something romantic for the TV cameras."

"What TV cameras?"

"At the library dedication."

She took a big swallow of champagne and felt sick.

"I think we should end this right now."

"No chance, Brenda. My store managers have gone to a lot of trouble publicizing and advertising your visits. You're not letting me down now."

"I will unless you promise this won't happen again."

"Nothing did happen," he said dryly.

"You know what I mean—coming here."

"You're saying you'll walk out on the tour if I come into your room again?"

"Something like that."

"Something or exactly?"

"Exactly!"

She didn't want more champagne, but she felt a compulsion to do something. A big gulp seemed to back up, burning her throat.

"Agreed," he said.

"Agreed?" He'd given in too easily.

They killed off the bottle in silence.

"I promise not to invite myself into your room again," he said somberly, saying each word with the precise diction of someone who's been drinking very fast.

"Then I'll finish the tour."

"Which you agreed to do anyway."

She felt terrible and couldn't get rid of him quickly enough. Walking to the door, she held it open.

"I take it you want me to leave now," he said dryly, pushing the cart toward the hall. "Very well."

Lulled by his agreement, the last thing she expected was his sudden move, taking her in his arms with ferocity. At first his kiss was an assault, ravishing her mouth and throwing new fuel on a fire that still glowed with white-hot intensity. When her hands fluttered against his back, he crushed her against him, anger and frustration welding them together. She opened her mouth, breathlessly receiving his kisses, clutching at his back and sinking in a quicksand of desire.

As abruptly as he'd kissed her, he released her, retreating to the hall and pushing the cart in front of him.

"I hope you regret this agreement as much as I do." He closed her door with an angry thud.

Making a sling of the large motel towel, he worked it angrily across his shoulders and down his back, not stopping until his firm buttocks glowed pinkly and the backs of his legs felt chafed. Wouldn't it be great if he could sluff off that woman as easily as he did dry skin! He felt a moment of savage relish as he thought of upending her over his knee and dusting her buns with a few well-deserved swats. Whipping the towel angrily across the edge of the tub, he knew he was kidding himself. The last thing he wanted to do to Brenda was hit her. He wanted to hold her, touch her, taste her, bury himself in the warmth he'd only begun to explore.

Thoughts he couldn't turn off brought a film of perspiration to his skin even as he paced naked in the cool room. Half a bottle of champagne hadn't washed away the taste of her mouth, and he had about as much chance of going to sleep as he did of flying out the window.

Why me? Why her? His thoughts raced furiously,

and he wasn't even sure he could stick to their agreement for one night, let alone three weeks.

After his divorce he'd decided to keep women on the fringes of his life; all he wanted was uncomplicated sex and occasional companionship. Both were easy to find, so why was he up-tight about striking out with Brenda?

Their rooms were connected by a set of double doors that had to be unlocked from inside each room. He unlocked the door on his side, only to face the solid expanse of brown varnished wood leading to Brenda's room. He knocked softly, so sure she wouldn't respond that he hated himself for making the gesture.

How could a woman who wrote realistic, sensual love stories be so reluctant to make love to him? He knew from her first responses to him tonight that she was attracted to him. So what was the problem? He wasn't used to failure, but his honest nature made him admit he could be at fault. He'd botched the trip idea from the beginning, not thinking straight when he went to her agent and publisher instead of discussing it some more with her. She had reason to be angry, but no one stayed angry forever. He'd restrained himself, barely touching her in New York and giving her two days on the road to get over her anger.

He turned on the TV, idly flipping stations, no more interested in what was playing than he was in spending three weeks at autograph parties. Her tour would be good for business, but it certainly didn't require his personal attention. Damn it, he had a corporation to run! Murray probably botched the deal in Canada, and the Loop store in Chicago needed immediate attention. The auditors hadn't turned up anything irregular, and the computerized inventories seemed to be in order, but something was wrong there. He'd probably have to fire the manager and possibly even the district manager. Maybe he'd run the store himself for a short time just to keep his hand in at the retail level. A store of that size should be showing a big profit, not just scraping by. He cursed himself silently. He should have known enough not to rearrange his life for any woman.

He was being ridiculous, and thinking about her wasn't helping. Sure, she was intelligent and beautiful. So were lots of women. But her shyness and vulnerability made him want to look after her and protect her. He hadn't felt this way about a woman in a long, long time.

He slammed his palm against the wall, wanting to batter down the door that separated him from Brenda. In spite of his long, sudsy shower, he still imagined the scent of her body trapped in the pores of his fingers, and it was driving him wild. If he didn't get over this sexual lunacy soon, he'd be thinking about a house in the suburbs, wedding bells, baby carriages, all the trappings of domestic disaster that had burned him once before. What he needed was a night with the lady author, so he could get her out of his system. He hadn't discovered any startling differences in women between the sheets, and he was too old to believe that forbidden fruit was sweeter.

"There has to be a cure," he said under his breath.

There was nothing in their agreement about bringing her to his room. . . .

Curled on the bed in a knot of misery, Brenda was still thinking about the noise she'd heard on the other side of the double doors that connected her room to Eric's. The sound of what might have been a knock had startled her, and she hadn't dared to hope he'd actually want to see her again tonight. She'd dashed toward the connecting door and waited anxiously for a second rap to confirm that Eric did indeed want to speak to her. Now she thought maybe she'd imagined the sound; maybe it had been an accidental bump, because waiting

94

by the door she'd heard nothing. And she hadn't dared to open the door on her side. It was no use lying in bed; she could no more sleep than she could cast a magic spell on Eric. He wanted her. Oh, yes, he wanted to sleep with her. His desire had branded her, his fingers searing the soft flesh he possessively fondled. But a woman had to be made of tougher stuff than she was to let a man into her heart for only a few nights. And she'd known from their first meeting that his charm was a gift he bestowed lavishly on all women. A divorced man who wanted new ties wouldn't still be single; his ex-wife had remarried and had two more children. Eric might be intrigued by the woman he'd glamorized for the tour, but she knew getting involved with him would only bring her pain.

Call it research, her inner voice urged. Would it be so terrible to spend a few nights with Eric? She would be inspired by a marvelous lover. How can a writer put feeling into love scenes if those in her life were only a faint memory?

She tried to imagine Eric without his clothes. Would his navel be cute and round, the size of her little finger? Was he ticklish? Would he like it if she squeezed his bottom and teased the little hollow at the end of his spine? How would his legs feel wrapped around hers, coarse or silky, heavy or sleek? Would she dare tell him that kissing the back of her neck made her wildly excited?

Was she going to torture herself this way all night? The room was still frigid, never having warmed up after her silly use of the air conditioner. She snuggled more deeply under the covers, pulling the sheet and nylon-edged green blanket under her chin. She was used to sleeping alone, and a few nights with Eric would only make it harder to go back to the solitary life she'd created for herself. No amount of rationalizing could change the facts: an affair with Eric Sheffield could only bring pain and disappointment. He didn't pretend to love her, and he wasn't offering her more than a publicity tour. *I'm not going to be a blooming idiot and fall for the wrong man,* she kept repeating to herself until she fell into welcome slumber.

Some motels had NO SMOKING accommodations; why not a NO PHONING room? She groggily reached for the receiver of the ringing telephone.

"Breakfast in half an hour?" Eric asked in a neutral tone.

"I need a little more time than that." Regaining her composure would take a lot longer than her morning routine.

"Forty-five minutes?"

"At least an hour. Why don't you go without me?"

"I have a better idea. I'll order room service."

Had he completely forgotten their agreement?

"No, please don't, Eric."

"Breach of contract, I guess," he said, no trace of bitterness in his tone.

"You did agree."

"Not to come to your room. Yes, I know." He wasn't going to point out the loophole in their agreement just to have breakfast with her. "I'll go alone, then. I do have quite a few calls to make before we check out."

"Only one bookstore today?" She tried not to sound too pleased.

"Just one. Our last stop in Pennsylvania. Do you want to meet me in the lobby at ten thirty?"

The closer to home, the safer she'd feel!

"Yes, I'll be there."

She met Eric on schedule, managing to avoid his eyes while they loaded the car and got on the highway. Tomorrow, she realized, she had to give a speech; the trip was going from bad to worse.

CHAPTER SIX

"Benedict, Ohio, Conduit Capital of the World," Eric said, finally spotting a parking place on a tree-shaded residential street several blocks from the business district and the library. "If they want to keep the downtown alive, they'd better do something about parking."

"Are all your stores in shopping malls?"

"Most of them. People shop where they can park their cars without paying. Our biggest store as far as floor space goes is in the Loop in Chicago, and it's not doing as well as it should."

She tried to concentrate on what he was saying, but her panic was building like air pressure before a storm. Searching for a place to park, Eric had driven past the library, a dignified marble-front building with lazy-looking lions flanking the steep steps. The new annex was beside it, a long, low buff-colored brick addition, but she scarcely noticed it, all her attention riveted on the platform and bleachers assembled on the spacious lawn in front of the old building. When she'd written her short speech, she'd expected to give it in a book-filled room with a few Friends of the Library in attendance. Instead it looked as if the whole town would turn out!

Eric came around and opened the door for her, offering his hand to pull her up the sharply sloping lawn beside the curb. The street wasn't much different from several in Charlotte: turn-of-the-century homes of brick, stucco, and wood with ornate little windows in third-story attics, gingerbread trim, and cupolas on roofs. A powdery-white house with a round tower in front and a porch on two sides reminded her of Uncle Fred's, but not even the magnificent old maples, their roots chewing up the sidewalks in spots, made her feel at home. Within the hour she was going to stand in front of a mike and hear her words echo over an audience of strangers.

"We're a little early," Eric said. "Maybe there's some place we can get a cup of coffee near the library. Am I walking too fast?"

"A little." Baby steps would get her there too soon!

"Careful, you'll catch your heel in a rut."

They moved to the already-trampled grass on opposite sides of a particularly crumbly section of the sidewalk, Eric grumbling about the city being liable for lawsuits if they didn't do something about repairing it. It wasn't like him to go around finding fault, and she accepted the blame, figuring he had to let off a little steam somewhere.

Already people were beginning to find places on the gray bleachers, and Eric decided they should make her presence known to the committee in charge of the dedication. A man in overalls and a string tie carrying metal folding chairs onto the speakers' platform thought they might find the head librarian in the old building.

John Parker was easy to spot. He was darting from person to person, making checks on a clipboard, nervously brushing back the few strands of dark hair on his

99

yellowish scalp. His features were almost beautiful, exquisitely molded but too delicate for his long, gangly build. The sharp slope of his shoulders and the bony prominence of his collarbone couldn't be disguised by the new-looking pearl-gray suit.

"Miss Storm, so nice that you could be here." He checked his list, obviously so flustered by his responsibilities that he'd forgotten why she was there. "I'm sure we must have your books in our paperback collection. We depend on donations, but our patrons are very supportive, very supportive."

At least one person is as nervous as I am, she thought, but this is probably the highlight of his career, the opening of a wing he'd planned and worked for. She felt like a usurper, horning in on a very special event that had absolutely nothing to do with her.

"I don't belong here," she whispered urgently to Eric.

"Why?"

"All these people worked hard to build this. Why should a stranger butt in?"

He laughed gently. "Don't you know book people love authors? Having you here is frosting on their cake. A week from now the library addition will be old stuff, but they'll still be thrilled about seeing a famous author."

"I'm not famous!"

"We're working on it!"

"I need a drink."

"I'll ask."

"No, no, I'll find a drinking fountain. Every library has one near the children's room."

She followed a sign, carefully descending the marble steps with deep hollows worn in their surfaces by generations of young feet. The fountain barely dribbled a weak stream of water, and a wad of pink gum stuck on top of the spout made her decide she wasn't that thirsty. On impulse she wandered into the children's section of the library, absentmindedly returning the smile of a young woman with a swinging brown ponytail and flat black slippers.

The room smelled like a library, the slight dampness of the basement capturing the scents of book bindings, rubber cement, and the whiff of adventure. Her earliest, sweetest memories included this intoxicating odor, and she still couldn't enter an unfamiliar library without a tinge of excitement. She'd met so many of her dearest friends on the low shelves of Charlotte's children's department: Huckleberry Finn, Alice, Jo and Beth and Amy and Meg, dear animal companions like Lassie and Black Beauty, the Borrowers, even Nancy Drew, kept on the shelves by a wonderfully understanding librarian who knew how important it was to feed children's imaginations. She circled the carpeted room enjoying a mural of children in foreign costumes painted years ago in oil on the yellowing plastered walls, stopping in front of a reading circle with fat plastic pillows in bright red, orange, and blue, only reluctantly leaving this sanctuary.

More people were milling in the foyer, and it took her a minute to spot Eric leaning against a pillar, staring ahead without really seeing, tension etching a line across his forehead.

He doesn't want to be here any more than I do, she realized suddenly, startled by the expression of preoccupation on his face. His business was huge and demanding; he'd admitted he was a workaholic. Yet he was patiently escorting her from store to store, and accompanying her to appearances like this one. Was he that determined to make love with her? Or was she a challenge, a woman who said no when he was used to yes?

101

She wanted to run to him, cling to him, in this crowded public place, tell him how much she cared.

He'd probably laugh at her! Love to her meant sharing their lives, growing old together, building, planning, caring. If he even suspected her real feelings, he'd be more than eager to forget about the tour. Turning then, he looked in her direction, watching her so intensely he seemed to be memorizing her appearance.

"The mayor will lead the procession out to the platform. You'll sit between the head librarian and a local poet."

"Where will you be?"

"In the audience. This is your show."

She checked her purse to make sure her speech was there, taking out the sheets of motel stationery with her neatest printing double normal size.

"Are you going to read it?" he asked.

"I have to."

"No time to memorize?" He sounded skeptical, knowing she'd spent long hours alone in her room the previous evening. The night had passed so slowly for him he could have memorized the Constitution.

"Plenty, but I knew I'd forget it anyway when I'm out there in front of all those people." She took out the folded pages, again returning them to her purse. Trying to relax was like untying knots in cooked spaghetti.

His eyes narrowed, the tiny laugh lines deepening, as he studied her face, then her hands, one of them busily shredding a tissue.

"You've got stage fright," he said, making a statement of fact.

"That's for actresses!" Her laugh was too forced to put him off.

"I knew there was something on your face when you came up to get your award—damn! How dumb can I

102

be! You're terrified of getting up in front of an audience."

"I am not TERRIFIED!" She'd never been a very good liar.

"No? It doesn't bother you to speak in front of people?"

"I don't enjoy it."

"The understatement of the year! You look scared to death. But why? You're beautiful, charming. People love to look at you. What could possibly be so terrible about saying a few words to a bunch of people you don't even know?"

"You couldn't possibly understand! You're a marvelous speaker!" She turned away from him, clutching her purse against her midriff, trying to ease the churning in her stomach.

"Sweetheart, no one's expecting a State of the Union address from you. Just smile, and they'll fall in love with you."

If that's all it takes, why don't you fall in love with me? she thought miserably. "I couldn't even tell my kindergarten class about my new parakeet. I'm not a public speaker, Eric."

"Will it help if I go on stage with you?"

"I forgot to be nervous when you kissed me at the convention," she admitted, her head downcast.

"If that's all it takes . . ."

He stepped in front of her, slowly brushing his lips against her forehead. "I hate to see you upset about a little thing like this." His lips covered hers, teasing a hesitant response. "That's for good luck." He kissed her again much more forcefully, making her forget for a moment that anyone else existed. "And that was for me."

". . . such carryings-on." A woman's voice roused Brenda from her trance, and she found the speaker, a brittle-looking matron in a dark brown suit the color of overcooked pudding, her faded hair piled on her head in lacquered rolls.

"People are watching," she whispered to Eric.

"Does that bother you so much?"

She glanced from the pinched face of the woman to Eric's warm smile. "No, it really doesn't."

She offered her mouth to be kissed again, and he didn't disappoint her.

"You'd better wipe your mouth," she teased.

He did, staining a crisp white handkerchief while she replaced her lip coloring, using a tiny mirror and brush from her purse.

"Sorry about your handkerchief. I should've given you a tissue."

"I plan to put it under my pillow tonight," he said, grinning for her benefit, wondering how much longer he could keep his hands off the bouncy roundness of her bottom, more tempting than she could possibly realize under the silkiness of her new violet dress. He marveled at how different she looked from the first time he saw her. A naturally pretty, primly dressed writer had metamorphosed into a strikingly beautiful best-selling author. But he realized uncomfortably that no matter what she wore, or how she styled her hair, he would still find her the most desirable woman in the world.

He shook his head impatiently. There were a hundred things he should be doing instead of standing around at this disorganized small-town hoopla, but when he looked at Brenda, her blue eyes nervously scanning the crowd, he had a hard time remembering what they were. Sometimes he thought just holding her could change his life, feeling her small chin pressing against his chest, her cheeks soft and fragrant, her shoulders slim, her back arching down to round, creamy buttocks. . . .

He buttoned his suit jacket with unusual self-consciousness. If he didn't put a muzzle on his imagination, he'd have to wait out the program hiding behind a pillar. And as successful as she was, she really did seem to need him. He'd been an idiot! No wonder she had balked when he talked about TV and public appearances. He'd never experienced stage fright himself, but an actress friend of his had told him she vomited before every performance. It was no joke to people who suffered from it.

His fingers slipped between hers, holding her hand in a dry, warm grasp.

"You'll be all right," he said softly. "When it's over, we'll go celebrate."

"What about the bookstore?"

"I did schedule one this afternoon, didn't I? Sometimes I'm too efficient."

"You're good at being efficient," she agreed, smiling.

"I'm good at a lot of things."

"Modest too!"

"No, honest. I haven't stopped kicking myself for arranging things behind your back. Most authors I've met would've said yes automatically."

"Unfortunately I'm not one of them."

"Am I forgiven yet?"

When he focused all his attention on her, his eyes sweeping her face with contrition and longing, she could forgive him anything.

"Do you forgive *me?* I'm the one who's been a terrible ingrate, not appreciating what you're doing for me. You must have a million other more important things to do than haul me around."

"Not a million," he said, "and none more important." Not if he were ever going to get a good night's sleep again. Would a few weeks be enough to get those hazy-blue eyes out of his mind?

105

The participants were lining up as the high school band, released from classes for the occasion, played the Ohio State fight song, then a Sousa march. The symbolism behind the selections escaped Brenda, so she assumed they were performing the numbers they knew best. How comforting to be part of a large group, dressed in gilded red jackets, plumed hats, and black pants like every other member, not standing out like Santa Claus on the Fourth of July. Was this going to be the time when she really did get sick to her stomach onstage? Eric squeezed her hand reassuringly.

"Do you want me to sit on the platform with you?" he asked. "I can ask the custodian to bring another chair."

"I'm a big girl now," she joked weakly. "But I wouldn't mind knowing where you'll be."

He glanced out the door. "The stands are packed. No seats there. I'll stand by that big maple tree on the left. See it?"

"Yes, I'll meet you there when it's all over. Wish me luck!"

"The best!" And a little for me too, he added to himself.

The head librarian sorted out the participants, and Brenda got caught up in a flurry of introductions, feeling a little less like an interloper when one library board member said she'd read her latest book. Most of these people, she was pretty sure, had never heard of her.

The list of people to be thanked by the mayor, acting as master of ceremonies, was exceeded only by the number of people who had a few words to say. Why, why, why did they want her there? She'd never even heard of the town. From now on she was hiring a stand-in for public appearances!

The town poet, lean, hollow-cheeked, and dapper in a pinstripe suit, preceded her, reading a witty poem he'd

106

written about the frustrations of winning the town's vote for the new annex, gently ribbing everyone from the mayor to the Friends of the Library. She laughed along with the crowd, appreciating the snappy verses even though she didn't know any of the people. The mayor, looking even more rotund than he was in a plaid suit, laughed until tears ran down his face. After he patted them away with a red silk handkerchief from his lapel pocket, he introduced Brenda with a spate of flowery compliments that made her think he was talking about someone else. When he said her name, she felt as if she were glued to her chair.

"Ms. Brenda Storm," he repeated, having a little trouble with Ms., a title he seemed to reserve for out-of-towners.

Eric was terribly far away, but she saw his nod, knowing it was given in encouragement. Somehow she got to the microphone, which had been adjusted to the height of the poet, who was over six foot two.

She said "It's a pleasure to be here" three times, frantically trying to lower the mike, which obviously wasn't picking up her voice.

"I think you turned it off," the mayor whispered, finally coming to her rescue.

Her speech went from bad to terrible. Her hands were trembling so much that the crackly sound of rustling papers was picked up by the system, and she was so agitated she mixed up the name of the town, calling it Benedictine instead of Benedict. No one laughed at the flub. She was trying to tell the audience what a vital part the public library had played in her life but was sure she sounded maudlin. She made Miss Perkins, the tiny little woman who ran the Charlotte Library's children's department, sound like a flighty Mary Poppins. Brenda scrapped the rest of her carefully prepared speech and ended abruptly, leaving the listeners a bit confused. The applause didn't begin until she was back in her seat; then she suspected that Eric had started it.

A vein was throbbing in her left temple, and she swore never to sit on the same platform with a politician again. The mayor spent another two minutes thanking her for coming, more time than her whole speech had taken.

The program finally ended, and the whole scene broke up in chaos, participants scrambling off the platform and people on the bleachers scurrying toward the new building, where a tour and refreshments were available. She lost sight of Eric, but not of the tree, trying to move in that direction but not making much progress. Maybe people felt sorry for her after the bungled speech. Quite a few shook her hand and thanked her for coming.

Eric was in sight at last, and the crowd was flowing in the opposite direction, when the woman with the stiff hairdo and drab brown suit cut across Brenda's path, blocking any possible evasive move.

"I want you to know, Miss Storm," she said in a dry, clipped voice, "that I did not approve of your appearance here."

"Oh?"

"I've been a member of the Friends of the Library for thirty-two years, and I've always striven to uphold the highest literary standards in this community."

"If you'll excuse me," Brenda said, ineffectively trying to sidestep the barrier of the woman's body, instinctively knowing what was coming.

"I feel I must say this on behalf of a great, great number of concerned citizens. Your flagrant exploitation of sex in your books is unacceptable to us, Miss Storm. When I was a girl, our reading was uplifting, not debasing."

"I'd never try to compare my writing to the best authors available in your day—D. H. Lawrence, James Joyce . . ." A lousy speaker she might be, but a doormat, never!

The woman's nostrils actually did flare; she'd have to remember that if she ever included a witch in one of her books.

"I would not read THAT kind of writing." She seemed about to flounce off, then changed her mind and launched another major attack. "Loose, lewd girls running after men. That's not what I call romance! The sacredness of our homes and families is threatened by the filth you write!"

"Have you read any of my books?"

"I hardly find that necessary. The cover tells me enough. I don't know what this country is coming to. Encouraging women to submit to all kinds of beastly things."

"Do you have children?"

"I have a fine, upstanding son."

"If he chose not to marry, would you want him to live as a celibate, never knowing what love is?"

"My son is married to a lovely girl who knows her place!"

"What is her place?" She knew that debating with this woman was an exercise in futility, but she didn't deserve this attack. She believed in love and wrote about deep, caring relationships. If that was evil, she didn't know the meaning of the word.

"You can be sure she has a hot meal on the table and a clean house for him when he comes home. She doesn't have time to read trash."

"Brenda, are you ready to go?"

Eric took her arm and guided her away, softly saying, "It's not worth it."

"Did you hear her?" She was torn between laughing

and crying. "Next she'd blame me for the buildup of nuclear weapons."

"Forget her. If you feel good about your work, nothing else matters."

"She made it sound like pornography!"

"She's read all your books, has she?" He put his arm around her shoulders and pulled her close.

"None, she says."

"She says?"

Brenda giggled. "Maybe she's a closet reader."

"Stranger things are true."

"She could be a romance addict trying to blame someone for her habit."

"I can see her hiding them from her husband," Eric said, laughing. "Under her bed. In a cabinet behind her best dishes."

"Maybe she has a loose floorboard in her bedroom."

"Which she undoubtedly occupies alone!"

They laughed so hard Brenda's conscience pricked her. "We shouldn't make fun of her, awful as she is. She probably had a repressed childhood."

"No, we should let her tar and feather you. Or maybe accuse you of sorcery. Has Ohio ever had a witch hunt?"

"You're terrible!"

"Sometimes I am. Let's give the old crone something to talk about for years."

He scooped her against him, heedless of the few curious people still wandering away from the library lawn, kissing her until she gasped for breath.

"Eric!"

"Let her enjoy this too."

Lacing his fingers into her hair, he planted warm kisses on her cheek and ear, oblivious to the spectators passing on either side.

110

"Now stop." Her protest was husky but weak. "I'll never dare come back to this town."

"Yes, I'd better stop before we get arrested." Locking his arm around hers, he hurried toward the car. "Your face is red."

"Yours should be!"

"I seem to remember a scene in your book . . ."

"No more commentaries on my writing!"

"Mine are all positive."

He was walking fast, ignoring the ragged cement of the sidewalk after they turned off Main Street.

"I've had enough of being an author today."

"What would you like to be?" He stopped abruptly and drew her into his arms again.

"Away from here for a start."

"No argument there." He clasped her hand and picked their way a little more carefully over slabs of loose pavement.

They were both a little breathless when they got back in the car.

"I'm really sorry about that." He sat behind the steering wheel and gripped it with both hands.

"It wasn't your fault."

"I should've found out how much you hate public speaking before I barged ahead and arranged things."

It was hard to argue with that.

"But you couldn't know the town dragon would attack me."

"You handled her well."

"I've had practice. The president of one of my mother's clubs crosses the street to avoid me now. That was one of the nice things about being at the convention—no, you don't want to hear this."

"I do," he said, meaning it sincerely.

"Everyone at the convention thinks it's wonderful to

111

write love stories. No one talked about censoring them or called them romantic drivel."

"People still do that?"

"A few. Even more ask me how much I make on each book."

"That bothers you?"

"Do strangers come up to you and ask what your annual income is?"

He laughed. "Good point. No, they don't. Only my accountant and the IRS know for sure. I have an idea."

"I'm afraid to hear it." Her smiled belied this.

"You deserve to have the rest of the day off."

"You did arrange another book signing."

"Yes, but I can cancel it."

"Readers may come and be disappointed."

"I'll tell my manager to give a free copy of your book to anyone who asks why you aren't there."

"Eric, I don't mind autographing books. Meeting readers is fun."

"It's settled. Sometimes I forget that people shouldn't work seven days a week."

He stopped at a service station for gas and made several calls, returning to the car with a smirk on his face.

"I feel like a kid playing hookey again," he said.

"Was that something you did a lot?"

"Twice. The first time when I was about eight."

"Did you get caught?"

"Did I!" He laughed and started the car. "It was late spring, a week or two before summer break. I got the bright idea of beating all the other kids to the golf course to hunt for lost balls. The pro at the country club used to buy them from us to use as practice balls."

"You were an enterprising little boy."

"Wasn't I!" He made a right turn back toward the expressway. "I found enough to nearly fill a pillowcase.

112

It was the best picking of my young life, let me tell you."

"And you made your first fortune?"

"Wrong. My father was out playing the course with some business associates and caught me. Among other things, he made me dump the whole lot back into a ravine. My profit for the day was one sore bottom. I can still see all those golf balls lying there for some other kid to claim."

"Well, that seems fair. Ill-gotten gains. It didn't discourage you from skipping school again?"

"No, the second time I took an unscheduled vacation from boarding school to help a friend harvest and haul Christmas trees."

"And got caught again?"

"Yeah, but I was too old to spank and I'd already invested my earnings in stock. Since I was determined to get rich on my own, Dad sent me to his father for a year. I did every dirty job my grandfather could find for me in his Texas oil fields."

"How old were you?"

"Seventeen. He wanted me to quit school for good and be a wildcatter like him. Instead I took a high school equivalency test and went on to college."

"You never graduated from high school?"

"I was in a hurry then. I had to have it all right away —a degree, a business, a wife."

"I'm impressed."

"Don't be. I owe my business to my grandfather's nose for oil, and I never took time to be a full-time husband."

"My father runs a retail business," Brenda said, thinking it was the safest way to respond to his confession. "I know there's more to succeeding than securing the capital you need to begin."

"What kind of business?"

113

"A hardware store in Charlotte. He had me sorting screws and dusting stock before I was ten."

"Child labor?"

"Hardly! I begged to go to the store with him. He started me at ten cents an hour, and I still go in and help out once in a while if he's shorthanded. I can figure how many sheets of paneling it takes to remodel a room and how many feet of tubing to modernize the plumbing."

"I always knew you were multitalented! Does your mother work in the store too?"

"She used to. Now she has a small craft store of her own. Yarn, art supplies, kits, things like that. They're both happier with separate businesses."

"I'm all in favor of that."

"Where are we going?" Maybe it was time she paid a little more attention to where this man was taking her.

"I thought we'd meander."

"Meander?"

"Turn off at the first promising country road and drive until we see a place we like. The rest of the day is ours."

And what a day it was! As if noticing spring for the first time, she drank in the grassy scent of the country air, letting a warm breeze whip her hair into a tangled halo. Trees and bushes along the road were sprouting brilliant foliage in a thousand different shades of green, making her sure no artist had ever captured such vibrant color with paint.

"You like my idea?" He lowered his window all the way as she had, breathing deeply.

"I love it. Can we have a picnic?"

"Great suggestion." Better than any he'd come up with, he thought, imagining an isolated clearing in the woods.

"There's a sign." She read aloud. "Comstock Crossing. Doesn't that sound like a village with a stream running through it? My instinct tells me they'll have a lovely place to picnic. A nice little park with picnic tables and a playground."

"I'll follow your instinct." He flicked on the turn signal, slowing down to exit.

After they passed a pair of gas stations and a short string of fast-food places, the road became curvy and hilly, deserted except for a yellow pickup truck going in the opposite direction.

"Does your instinct tell you this road goes somewhere?" he teased.

"Look. That sign says Comstock Crossing seven miles."

The road got steeper. It was paved but still got dusty when a decrepit farm truck came toward them heading in the direction of the highway. They passed an orchard, the low twisted branches heavy with fluffy flowers, some already falling like pink snow. The farms had weathered gray barns and turn-of-the-century homes flanked by tumble-down out buildings and agricultural equipment in various stages of rust.

"We've found the real rural scene, I guess." He wondered if he'd have to contend with backwoods boys out shooting squirrels.

"You can't judge a farm by the buildings," she said. "Farmers hate to spend money on home improvements. My sister renovated her centennial home practically single-handedly."

"Centennial home?"

"It's been in her husband's family for over a hundred years. She would've come with me to New York, but their barn burned down."

"Did they lose any animals?"

"No, they just grow corn and soybeans."

"Your only sister?"

115

"Yes, and no brothers."

"I have a younger brother. He's a partner in my father's law firm."

Comstock Crossing was the kind of town she might've invented for a romantic afternoon. Tulips bloomed in the gardens and the yards of small neat bungalows and older frame houses were tended with loving care. Bushes had white and yellow blooms popping from their buds, and more than one white picket fence shadowed the tips of lavender and pink crocuses. The flowery perfume in the air was tranquilizing, making her think of dozing on a grassy knoll. The few townspeople moving about seemed to be savoring the day, storing up its sweetness to last through the sticky hot days of summer, going about their tasks in slow motion so they could prolong their time in the fresh air.

"There's exactly what we want," Eric said, sounding a little excited.

A white-washed replica of a windmill perched on the green shingled roof of a small restaurant, and behind it neat little tourist cabins were strung out in four short rows.

"We can get a picnic lunch here," he said.

They left the restaurant loaded with triple-layer sandwiches on homemade bread, thick slices of blueberry pie wrapped in foil, and coffee in a thermos they promised to return. A pink-cheeked little man who worked behind the counter had given them directions to Goshen Park a half mile west on Cumberland Road, County 270.

Heavy, long picnic tables were clustered around blackened outdoor grills and a clear stream ran alongside them. The play area for children looked newly spruced up for spring. The steel pipes of the swing set gleamed like oversized silver Crayolas. A sand pit enclosed by two-by-fours formed a bright yellow square

116

filled with a fresh load of fine white sand. An old-fashioned teeter-totter was coated with fresh, still sticky-looking green paint, and whimsical horses grinned on their spring pedestals. It was just the kind of park Brenda had loved as a kid.

"We have the place to ourselves, it seems," he said.

"Do you think those clouds are rain clouds?"

"No, it won't rain on our picnic. I wonder what's on the other side of the stream. There's a little footbridge down there."

"We could eat here first and go wading later," Brenda suggested. "You know what I love? Walking through sand with bare toes."

"I'll push you on the swings if you like, but let's eat first. I'm starved."

"So am I. Do you like that table by the big spruce?"

"No, just to satisfy my curiosity, let's see if there're any tables on the opposite side." He rested his free hand lightly on her waist.

"You're more curious than hungry?"

He was more something than hungry.

"Wonderful day, except for being a little overcast." He kept his hand on her waist, guiding her toward the small wooden footbridge.

"It may be private property."

"They wouldn't build a bridge if the park didn't extend to the other side."

The weathered planks creaked underfoot, but there was no threat in their protest. Beneath, the water was crystal clear, polishing stones and boulders in the streambed into gemlike smoothness, the pinks, tans, and grays sheltering an occasional iridescent flash of silvery scales.

"A boy's dream, fishing a stream like this."

"Are you a fisherman?" she asked.

"No, I'm not patient enough." He couldn't believe

the patience he had with this lovely, elusive woman. Was she really naïve enough to believe he wanted to picnic?

"Catching a fish isn't the important thing." She stopped on the far side of the bridge and stared into the stream. "It's being in the woods with the water singing to you and birds flashing their tails in the treetops."

"The catch isn't fun?"

"Of course it is, but it's a bonus. The real pleasure is just being there."

Being with her was a pleasure too, a puzzling, frustrating joy that made him want to prolong their outing indefinitely. "I still like something to show for my time," he said.

"A trophy?" She moved ahead of him on the steep bank of grass skirting the woods, wondering if he wanted to add her to his collection.

"No, just a sense of accomplishment."

"You can't enjoy just being in a beautiful natural place?"

"I can when I'm with you." He was surprised to realize how much he meant it.

"I don't see any tables on this side. The bank's too steep."

"Let's wander in the woods a little."

"That box must be heavy."

"Not at all."

"The ground is probably damp this early in the season."

"The soil looks sandy. I imagine it's well-drained." He captured her hand, caressing the dry smoothness of it with his fingers.

"Watch out for ground roots. There doesn't seem to be a clear path," she warned.

"Sure there is. I imagine people walk this way all the time in the summer." Lovers, he wanted to say.

"The trees are getting thicker." She pulled her hand away and looked back toward the stream.

"Are you afraid?"

"Of course not." Not of the woods, she almost added.

"See, high and dry." He stepped into a tree-shaded clearing, the new growth of forest vegetation still velvety soft underfoot, as inviting as a golf green.

"It is lovely."

Her heels were sinking into the soft turf, but the woody aroma of pine resin and budding oaks was clouding her judgment. It was the kind of clearing that should be peopled by tiny elves under newly sprouted mushrooms or fairies tiny enough to ride humming-birds.

He sneezed, kicked off his shoes, and took off his jacket, sinking down to sit Indian-style on the natural blanket of the forest, spreading their makeshift feast on paper napkins.

Following his lead, she removed her pumps, tucking nylon-clad toes under her knees when she crossed her legs, glad the dress she was wearing had a full skirt. "Does the budding make you sneeze?"

"No. Here, the sandwiches look drippy." He leaned forward to tuck a paper napkin under the neckline of her dress.

"I haven't worn a bib in ages."

"These sandwiches have everything—mayo, mustard, relish, lettuce, tomatoes. I count four kinds of cold cuts and three kinds of cheese."

"We won't need dinner."

"No, we won't need that." He bit into a thick sandwich, proving that he was the one who needed a bib when a stream of tomato seeds and juice squirted out.

"I warned you, didn't I?" he said, laughingly taking another bite.

"Tomato stains. You should rinse it right away."

"I'll do that in the stream when we start back." He crumpled a napkin and slipped out of his shirt, laying it aside.

"It's not warm enough to go shirtless, not with the sky so cloudy," she said, keeping her eyes on her sandwich, trying to keep the squashy layers together, not wanting to see the smooth swell of his shoulders or the dark sprinkling of hair that disappeared under his waistband. The compact firmness of his torso didn't surprise her; the way she felt about it did. She ached to lean forward and trace the dark circles of his nipples, to feel the inviting warmth of his chest cradling her. The bite of bread and tomato in her mouth couldn't fill the emptiness she felt in her heart.

Slowly and quietly they nibbled at their sandwiches, wrapping the remains in the plastic wrap, sipping coffee from styrofoam cups and pretending they were too full for pie.

"It's quiet here today."

"Not if you listen," she said. "The birds are nesting. They resent our intrusion."

"You're imagining that."

"No, I'm not." What she was imagining brought patches of scarlet to her cheeks, making her fidget restlessly, stretching her legs out away from him, avoiding his eyes.

Staring off into the woods, she didn't see him move, but his breath was warm on the back of her neck, his hand brushing aside the soft curls clustered there. With a tenderness known only to lovers and poets, he ran his lips along her hairline, nibbling and kissing until her nerve endings sent lightning bolts of longing down her spine. Turning toward him to save her sanity, she met his mouth with parted lips, drawing his tongue between the slick edges of her teeth.

Rising to their knees, they pressed their bodies together, breathing in ragged spurts as their cheeks quivered under the impact of long, demanding kisses. She couldn't control his hands when hers were tentatively exploring the smooth skin of his shoulders, the sensuous curve of his spine, the slight softening of his midriff below the hard pads of his chest.

"Touch me," he said softly, steadying his hands with difficulty to undo the slippery little buttons at the back of her dress.

Stroking his chest, she shivered when her bra parted in back and the dress slid to her waist. His hands cupped her breasts, stroking them so tenderly she wanted to weep with joy.

"So nice," she whispered, hugging his hands against them.

"I want everything to be nice for you," he promised solemnly, touching her even more gently until she ached for the firmness of his mouth on her erect nipples.

He eased her backward, torn between a pounding need to penetrate her and an even more compelling desire to bring her happiness. He felt her writhe under the skilled ministrations of his tongue and parted her legs to make room for his knee. With her breath escaping in gasps and blood pounding in his ears, he felt his control slipping away, wanting to rip off her panties and lose himself in her depths. Instead he loosened his slacks, sliding down the zipper, hoping against hope that she'd take him, want him. Her little-girl petting was driving him crazy as her fingers slid over his torso with a timidness that was maddening but erotic. Neither of them noticed the few tiny drops of rain that pelted their feverish skin.

Inside she was weeping, wanting him but craving even more to hear that he loved *her,* not the glamorous woman Andre had created in his salon. Eric was a magician, using his whole body to make her wild and wanton, but where would it end? "So long, it's been good to know you?" She felt her body go limp, not because she willed it but because the fear of loving him and then losing him terrified her. Here they were tussling in a public park like—like people in love. Only Eric wasn't in love with her. Not even now, in the heat of passion, did he pretend to love Brenda Storm, the person.

Was he hurting her? Pushing her too fast? She'd been as eager as he was, but now he'd lost her. He laid his hand between her legs, feeling a telltale throbbing under the soft material of her panties, but she was backing off, wishing him away. He kissed her mouth, a long, hard kiss that she neither resisted nor returned. If he wanted her, it had to be now, before she slipped away completely. Her body remained passive as he peeled off her panties, but he made a terrible mistake: he looked into her eyes.

"Darling, if you don't want to?" The question made his throat ache.

"I do, but . . ."

"But?"

"It's starting to rain."

"A few drops won't hurt us." He sneezed loudly.

"Bless you. We'd better go."

"No."

"What then?"

"Let me love you."

"It's too soon. Too fast." She couldn't tell him that she'd do anything, anytime, anywhere, if only he'd say that he loved her a little. "If we don't leave now, we'll get soaked."

"I understand." He didn't, and the calm, accepting voice that answered her seemed to belong to someone other than Eric.

She looked as miserable as he felt as larger drops of rain were absorbed in the silky darkness of her hair. All

122

he wanted was to hold her, cherish her, but her expression was making him feel like a heel.

"Let me." She touched him the way he'd wanted, knowing he had every right to be disappointed, desperately wanting to give him satisfaction even if her heart wasn't in it.

"No." His refusal was only a hoarse croak. If she touched him again, something might happen that he'd regret even more than bringing her on this tour in the first place. "I'm going to rinse my shirt now."

"Yes," she said dejectedly.

She dressed as quickly as possible, distressed because her fingers had forgotten how to do the simplest things, fumbling with her side zipper until she managed to concentrate her full, undivided attention on fastening it. She wanted desperately to go home and forget all about Eric and the way he made her feel.

The stream was frigid, and his socks and the bottoms of his pants legs were soaked, clinging to his ankles and peppering his flesh with goosebumps without appreciably cooling his ardor. The damn spots weren't going to come out with the little handkerchief sponging; all he had to show for bounding into the stream were wet clothes and a bruised toe. Rain pelted his forehead, and he slipped going up the steep bank, banging his knee and getting dirt and grass stains on his slacks. He'd throw them and the shirt away; he wanted no souvenirs of this afternoon! His Chicago store was going down the tubes, and here he was making a fool of himself, relentlessly pursuing the author Brenda Storm, whom he thought was the loveliest female to fall his way in a lifetime. He should drop the tour today, but . . . But what? Was he afraid he couldn't forget her if he left things as they were? He fought his way up the slippery slope. He knew he'd continue the tour with her but he didn't know why.

"Are you ready to go?" He could see she was; every last scrap of paper was packed in the box.

"You're wet."

"Yes, and dirty. I slipped."

"Are you all right?" It wasn't the mud and rain that concerned her.

"Of course." He sounded a little cranky; his feelings couldn't be shut off like a faucet.

"Sorry I asked." Sorry for more than that, she thought miserably.

"Let's go."

"Yes."

They made a run for the car, thudding across the wooden bridge, made slippery by what was now a deluge. Her dress was plastered to her body, and rain streamed down her face from her soaked hair. She reached over the seat and found her raincoat in the back, but it was too late for it to do more than keep the seat dry. She was shivering with cold, and Eric looked worse than she felt, sneezing convulsively until his face was scarlet.

"We'd better find a place to stay," he said, not liking the scratchy feeling in his throat.

"Maybe those cabins by the windmill restaurant."

"Might as well try there. We promised to return their thermos."

The man in the restaurant also rented the cabins.

"I only have one left. Wilkins family's havin' a big reunion. Took all but number six for the out-of-town folks. Come from Toledo, Cincinnati, far away as Davenport. Big family."

"We need two," Eric insisted, sneezing and shivering at the same time.

"How far to the nearest motel?" Brenda asked.

"Thirty, forty miles, I reckon. But a lot of salesmen stop there, so who knows if there's a vacancy."

124

"We'll take number six," Brenda said with resignation, accepting the metal ring with a key dangling from it.

"Only to change clothes and dry off," she said as they drove the car back to the cabins.

"Whatever you say," Eric agreed.

The cabin was knotty pine inside, a single small room with a double iron bedstead painted white. The bathroom was tiny with no tub, just a shower stall, but someone had put a great deal of thought into decorating the place. The curtains and quilt were certainly the products of a home sewing machine, with big squares of gingham in yellows, blues, and reds sewn together. The rug on the floor was hand-braided in a dozen shades of yellow and blue, and the nightstand and small dresser had crocheted white doilies. The single painting in the room was obviously a paint-by-number copy of a famous still life and its natural pine frame was yellowed with age. Even the yellow towels had W.C. for Windmill Cabins embroidered on them instead of the usual stamped motel markings. They smelled like they'd been laundered and dried with a fabric softener in someone's home.

"It's cozy," Eric said, peeling off his soaked jacket.

"You can use the shower first. You sound like you're coming down with a cold."

"Thanks." He looked around for a place to put his damp clothes, found a miniature closet, and hung up his jacket and shirt.

The shower seemed extraordinarily loud, or maybe it was the rain battering their small refuge that made the room sound like it was under Niagara Falls. Eric seemed to take forever, finally coming out with a towel secured around his waist. She caught only a glimpse of muscular calves before ducking into the bathroom, a pile of dry clothes in her arms. She didn't hurry. If they

125

were paying for the room for the night, they might as well use it for a few hours.

The bathroom was still steamy from Eric's shower, but it was clean and the water was hot. She stood under the spray a long time, trying not to think about the picnic and the way she felt when Eric touched her.

It wasn't that the tour made her resent Eric. She was afraid of him, scared that he'd make her care too much, then drop her. What she needed in her life right now was security, permanence, lifelong companionship. With Eric these things seemed hopelessly out of reach.

She dressed in the moisture-filled cubicle and towel-dried her hair, letting it fall in natural ringlets to her shoulders instead of teasing it into the sleek waves Andre had insisted were more flattering. Her hope that Eric was ready to leave was forgotten when she saw him under the quilt, soundly sleeping.

He didn't stir when she came close to the bed, and she couldn't bring herself to wake him. Asleep, he seemed much more boyish, his hair tousled and his eyelids fringed by long, fine lashes. Lying on his side facing her, he'd pushed aside the covers so one arm and shoulder were bare, the skin firm and smooth over muscular contours. Brenda instinctively pulled the covering higher, remembering how cold he'd been.

What harm could there be in letting him nap? There was plenty of time to find separate accommodations after he slept awhile. She was sleepy too, and if the only upholstered chair was too low-backed for comfort, she could at least relax with a paperback until he awoke.

The book fell from her hands and her head slumped forward, but she remembered only that the words were swimming on the page. Awaking suddenly in her awkward position, she was surprised that more than an hour had passed. Eric was still sleeping, stretched out on his back with the quilt pushed down to his waist. A little stuffy snore told her he'd probably wake up with a dilly of a cold, especially if he was still chilled. She moved cautiously to the bed, narrow for a double, and tried to inch up the quilt without waking him. She didn't succeed.

Capturing both of her hands, he opened his eyes and looked into hers, enchanted by the smoky blue depths, feeling something much more exciting than the lust that continually plagued him when she was near him. Part of what made her so beautiful was her unawareness of her own beauty. Her innocence was soul-deep, the kind that would grow into compassion and deep love if she gave it a chance. Suddenly he needed to hold her more than he needed to breathe, pulling her down on his chest and holding her there, feeling the beat of her heart and hearing her muffled protest.

For once Brenda ignored her common sense and lay silently in his arms, her cheek pressed against his shoulder. His bare skin still smelled soapy from the shower, and she was fascinated by the one flaw on his arm, a vaccination mark, a pale, pinched scar that she reached out to touch.

For a few long minutes the contentment of being close to each other was enough. But then he began to stroke her back through the candy-striped cotton blouse she'd changed into, and she began to caress his arm, tracing the veins in the hollow of his elbow and parting the hairs on his forearm with the tip of her little finger. They had the patience of very old friends and the wonder of very new lovers, drinking in pleasure from their intimacy.

He was going to kiss her, and thinking about it was almost as wonderful as doing it. He imagined her lips, soft and full, slowly parting under his gentle suckling. He wanted to run his tongue over the slippery ridges on the roof of her mouth and thrust it deeply into her mouth. He longed to fully arouse her, to see her nipples grow taut and her skin moist with the lubrication of love. Stunned by the satisfaction he felt in just holding her and imagining these things, he experienced a rush of strong emotion that had nothing to do with the demands of his masculinity. He cuddled her closer, holding her like a fragile, precious treasure, unwilling to make any move that would shatter this precious moment.

It felt so right to be in his arms, feeling his rhythmic breathing, nuzzling his chest. She was getting drunk without drinking, swooning without fainting. Afraid her head was growing heavy on his shoulder, she propped herself up on one elbow and looked at his face, seeing the tip of his tongue moisten his lips and his right eyebrow rise a little above the left. His eyes were dark and penetrating.

When they did kiss, their lips met tentatively. But when his tongue slipped into her mouth, she responded with urgency and found her heart pounding with the shock of pleasure. Never had all her senses been so alive, so stimulated.

He kicked aside the quilt, wanting her skin to touch his, and felt elated when she helped him strip off her blouse and bra. Trailing his fingers over her breasts, he tortured himself with denial, avoiding the rigid tips until she cupped his hands over them, her moan a primitive wail he never would have imagined coming from her.

Had she ever felt like this before, wanting so much that she was teetering on the edge of panic, afraid the reality could never meet her expectations? She forgot about keeping her thighs discreetly covered, forgot about the table lamp illuminating every contour of her body, forgot about caution, commitment, and consequences.

Her beauty, fully revealed after the rest of her clothing was removed, brought a painful lump to his throat, and he couldn't kiss her deeply enough. Exploring her with his lips and hands, he felt almost psychically attuned to what pleased her and what didn't.

She was as anxious to touch as she was to be touched, forgetting about the man who wore three-piece suits and made million-dollar decisions. The muscular compactness of his body thrilled her, and her hunger for him was like an addiction, raging and blinding.

He planned to be gentle and slow, to sweep her along on his own waves of passion, to give her enjoyment and satisfaction. What happened between them couldn't have been planned. It wasn't just that she wanted him; she became part of him. Tricks, techniques, pacing had nothing to do with the explosion of desire that rocked him as much as it did her. With other women he thought he was a good lover; with Brenda he didn't think at all.

The waves of sensation weren't totally unique, but sharing her climax so completely was. She didn't turn away and bury her face in a pillow to ride out her sensuality in mental solitude. Clinging to Eric, she moaned with joy, sharing it with him and loving him.

"You're wonderful," he whispered.

CHAPTER SEVEN

The light was blocked by the blue patches in the curtains but seeped through the red and yellow, filtered to a hazy orange, showing her the dim outlines of their mini-refuge, its furnishings concocted by someone with more time than money. Yesterday she'd seen the stains on the ceiling, the bare spots on the wooden floor where the varnish was worn, and the fine black line of dirt and mold edging the window glass. This morning her mood made the fading quilt and frayed rag rug seem cozy, even gay. She'd heard Eric leave the cabin but knew he'd soon be back.

His knock was soft and tentative. He wasn't sure if she was sleeping, but he wanted her to come to the door still groggy, her cheeks pink from the coarse cotton pillowcase, her hair an untamed mop of silky jet. The sheets would still be warm from her body, with the nose-tingling fragrance of her perfume clinging to them. He balanced two styrofoam cups of coffee in one hand, ready to use the key if he had to, but she didn't disappoint him.

She'd pulled on a nightgown to open the door, making him smile when he remembered how she'd hidden in

130

that damn tent of a raincoat. The filmy white gown clung to the perfect peaks of her breasts, magically revealing more than it concealed; luscious creamy curves and a suggestion of dark, secret places. Biting his lower lip, he gave himself a mental shake, a warning not to spoil this tenuous new relationship by rushing it.

Brenda wasn't at all sure what to say to him. If she'd written this scene, here would be the place for the hero to declare his eternal love. She'd throw open the door, and they'd rush into each other's arms. He'd shower her face with eager kisses. No, that always sounded too wet. He'd look into her eyes and say something about not being able to live without her. Oh, never mind, she thought impatiently. Even in her imagination she wasn't sure how she wanted this big scene to go.

"Good morning." He was still standing on the second of three wooden steps. "I don't remember seeing that gown last night."

"I pack one for emergencies like opening doors." She tried to sound humorous but it came out flip. Hold me, you idiot, she wanted to say.

"Sassy this morning." He moved inside, keeping his arms away from her by a supreme effort of will. "Here's coffee. I thought we'd drive awhile, then stop for breakfast."

"I don't drink coffee."

"Darling, I'm sorry. I forgot. Tea. I'll go get tea."

"No, not now." She wondered if he wanted to kiss her as much as she wanted to kiss him.

"Did you sleep well?" He glanced at the iron bedstead. He'd had better bunks at summer camp, but he'd never forget what he'd experienced on this one.

"Very, thank you. You?"

"Like a log. Fresh air and exercise does that to me."

Like hell it did! His toe was throbbing from stubbing it on a stone in the streambed, and he was definitely getting a head cold. If he wasn't feeling so wonderful, he'd be miserable.

She dressed in the bathroom; he packed and wished he had something for his head. It was so stuffy it ached. Fast dressing wasn't her specialty, apparently, and they had an autograph party two hours away. She could have told him that following all Andre's instructions took a big chunk of time in the morning.

Something needed to be said; they both sensed it but neither knew how to begin. He couldn't bring himself to ask something trite like "Was it good for you?" She had too much pride to try to maneuver him into making any kind of commitment. Was he trying to figure out how to let her know last night had only been a little recreation to him?

They ate breakfast at the Windmill. His toast was smothered in butter and jam, and her inch-thick waffle grew soggy under two more inches of blueberries and whipped topping. He finished only one piece of toast, drinking cup after cup of coffee while she picked at her food.

"I think we'd better talk," he said outside in the car.

About what, he wasn't sure, but a potful of brackish coffee had given him a sour stomach, and he wouldn't refuse a little sympathy for his cold. They were acting like strangers when he needed and wanted her warmth.

"This tour isn't what you expected," she said morosely, steeling herself for a "let's still be friends" speech.

His eyes, red-rimmed because of his cold, were impossible to read.

A semi pulled into the restaurant lot, making its vibrations felt as it narrowly missed their rear bumper. She turned to glimpse it through the back window, her mouth colliding with Eric's when she straightened her head. Accepting his first kiss with surprise and his sec-

132

ond with need, she clutched at the back of his head, weaving short strands of hair around her fingers.

"You see how it is," he said, his shoulders and head drooping when he turned from her. "I want to make love to you again, darling. I want you to sleep in my bed tonight."

It wasn't what she'd expected. "Our agreement . . ."

"Isn't working."

"No."

A truck driver walked in front of their car, pushing a greasy cap farther back on his head of faded red curls and staring at them with open curiosity. When the green and white plaid of his shirt disappeared into the restaurant, Eric leaned closer, slowly caressing her knee.

"Not here," she protested.

"In your book you didn't show any scruples about public displays of affection."

She pushed at his hand, not sure whether she was ready to explode with anger or pleasure. He withdrew it.

"We could go back to our cabin," he suggested tentatively.

"You scheduled two bookstores today."

"I don't give a damn about books!"

"Or about the tour?"

"Not right now, no." He reached for the key in the ignition, but she caught his hand in hers.

"I think we should go to them."

"That's a change of heart for you."

"You've convinced me. I was foolish not to jump at such a wonderful opportunity. I'm sorry."

"Any writer would be a damn fool to pass it up." He wanted to talk about them, not about stores and tours. If he crushed her against him right now, would she admit she wanted him?

It hurt to have her apology thrown back at her. "Be honest, Eric. You planned this tour because you thought I'd sleep with you."

"You make it sound like I was trying to buy you."

"What should I think?"

"We met. I was interested. The tour gives us time to get acquainted."

"And that's all you wanted?" She was aching to ask what would happen after it was over, but seeing the impassive expression on his face, she lost her courage.

"Visiting authors are good for my business. I told you that. They create excitement in the stores."

He never should have taken her to that glamour factory. Her natural beauty was enough to bring his heart to his throat. Debating with this lovely woman when his nose was running and his head throbbing was like asking Gonzilla to court Garbo. He'd definitely goofed; this wasn't the time for a serious talk, not when he wasn't sure what he wanted himself.

"How often has the president of Sheffield Bookshelves personally escorted a romance author on tour?" she asked.

"If you still want it to be strictly business, that's the way it will be." He was so angry he almost believed himself. Damn, but he felt lousy this morning.

"I'm sure that would be best," she said stiffly. It would be the best way to guarantee her misery. She was close to tears and hated her weakness.

"Let's go." He ground the starter in his impatience.

"I think I should go home, Eric."

"No."

"You can't stop me."

"I guess not, but do you realize how much I've got invested in this trip?"

"You can cancel most of the advertising."

"I suppose so."

134

"And the cardboard stand-ups of me."

"Not those."

"You can return the extra books."

"You agreed to this tour, Brenda."

"You agreed to stay out of my room."

"Have I broken my agreement?"

"Technically no, but . . ."

"If you're determined to quit, I'll drive you home."

"You have to visit your stores."

"No, I hire district managers to do that. The only one I really want to check in person is the Chicago store. I can take you home on my way there, but I won't drive straight through."

"Another night on the road. I'd rather get a bus."

"Brenda, you don't want to travel by bus. I'll leave you at an airport."

"No. I like riding buses. It gives me time to think."

"You may not believe it, but I really need you in Chicago. That store's in trouble. If I can't increase sales, I may have to close it."

"You're not going to pretend I can save an ailing store?"

"No, but it's not asking too much to expect you to keep the engagements I've scheduled for you."

He'd had more eye contact in a dentist's chair than he did with her during this conversation. Maybe she didn't want to quit any more than he wanted her to.

"And if I refuse?"

"It's your career."

"Is that a threat?"

"Call it whatever you like."

Driving without taking his eyes off the road, his hands felt glued to the wheel and his knuckles were white with tension. Pain was building over his right eye, and his head was so stuffy he could barely breathe. He

135

wanted to sleep around the clock, not force a showdown with Brenda.

"Why can't you just forget about promoting my books and take me to the nearest bus depot?"

"You can't believe I'd be happy about canceling your public appearances!" He sneezed, a muffled explosion that made his head pound. Digging out his handkerchief, it occurred to him that it was his last clean one.

"All of them made without consulting me!"

"That's what's really bothering you, isn't it? I trampled on your precious independence!"

"It doesn't matter now."

"No, it certainly doesn't." He sneezed again, wiping his eyes impatiently.

"Are you all right?"

"Perfectly!" Except he needed another handkerchief, a hot toddy, and twelve hours sleep.

"You've caught a spring cold. The worst kind. Here, take my pack of tissues. You shouldn't have waded in that stream."

"Oh, sh . . ." This time his sneeze erupted with such force the car jolted out of its lane, straying across the narrow blacktop until he forcefully turned the steering wheel.

"You can't drive like this! You'll get us killed!"

"Not us, me! You're hopping a Greyhound, remember?"

"Oh, pull over. I'll drive."

"I don't need your charity." He tossed the tissues back on her lap, keeping two fresh ones wadded in his hand.

"Don't tell me you're too macho to admit you're feeling lousy?"

"I feel lousy." He pulled onto the narrow gravel shoulder of the road, braking too hard, getting out and tramping through thigh-high weeds on the passenger

136

side of the car to relinquish the wheel to her. A steel band was tightening across his forehead, his nose was watering, and visions of hot rum sliding down his raspy throat brought a warm sheen to his face. Loosening his tie didn't help his breathing.

"You look feverish."

"It's just a little cold. If you want to drive, drive." He didn't say where.

"Fasten your seat belt."

She accelerated slowly, squinting against the glare of the sun, wishing she had her familiar compact car. His concentration on the road ahead was making her feel like a student under the watchful eyes of a drivers' training teacher, but once they reached the interstate he fell asleep, breathing noisily through swollen nostrils.

Highway 80 and the normalcy of the route west across the green swells of Ohio lulled her into a dangerously drowsy state, forcing her to stay awake by consciously probing wounds she preferred to let heal. Here was a classic romantic situation: the hero ailing, needing tender care, and the heroine tortured by her budding love for him. She'd used this dramatic device herself in a early, forgettable book. They'd stop at a motel where, of course, there was only one vacant room, and she couldn't possibly abandon him in his weakened condition. She'd have to undress him and bathe his fiery flesh with trembling white hands. Then chills would rack his virile masculine body; she'd risk her cherished virginity—no, scratch that—she'd press her trembling body—no, mustn't use "trembling" twice. She'd stretch her pulsating body against his and warm his cold flesh with her burning skin. Never mind that skin never burned; this line of thinking was making Brenda the Author more than a little hot.

Eric's stuffy snore and a mileage sign for Cleveland shifted her mind to more practical problems. She was

137

supposed to sign books in a couple of hours, she wanted to go home instead, and Eric really must have a whopper of a cold to sleep so soundly. Also the car needed fuel very soon. Exiting where a highway department sign assured her of the availability of gas, food, and lodging, she pulled into a station beside the full-service pumps and touched Eric's arm to wake him.

"Fill 'er up?" a scrawny young attendant asked.

"Yes, and check under the hood, please."

"Where are we?" He rubbed his eyes with the back of his hand and blinked against the brightness of the day.

"Still southeast of Cleveland. Shouldn't you call the bookstore or something?"

"Or something, I suppose. Do you have another tissue?" His voice was hardly recognizable, and he accepted the rest of her packet with a groan and a cough.

She watched him disappear inside the station; his gray suit jacket was wrinkled, and he moved without the usual spring in his step.

"What should I do now?" she asked when he finally flopped down beside her again.

"Drive, I suppose."

"Where?"

"I suggest west unless you have a better idea."

His nose was showing telltale tinges of pink, and the rims of his eyes were swollen. She had an irrational impulse to kiss him, germs or no germs, but she didn't.

"You know what I mean. I want to go home, Eric."

"I don't give a damn where you go. I'm going back to sleep."

A small sign indicated that Wallington Falls was a few miles down the road. Brenda paused in the station drive, impulsively reaching over to touch his forehead with the backs of her fingers. He did feel feverish, and she didn't have much to lose by zipping into town and buying some aspirin or maybe a cold remedy. They'd never gotten around to discussing his views on patent medicines, but she wished for some of her mother's lemon-honey-whiskey concoction to knock the rumbles out of his chest.

Eric hardly stirred when she left him in the car, hurrying into a small pharmacy with a striped green awning over the entrance. Inside, the store was larger than it looked, and it took her a few minutes to find the cold remedies on a side wall near the postal substation. After selecting two syrups and three bottles of pills to give him a choice, she went back to the car to show him the medicines. He was sound asleep again.

Skirting Cleveland, she drove until her throat was parched and her stomach noisy with hunger, worrying because Eric stayed asleep, groaning and coughing but not becoming fully conscious. He hadn't taken any of the medication she'd bought.

It wouldn't be hard to find a bus station in the populous area along Lake Erie, but what should she do about him? She couldn't just abandon him, not when he didn't seem to be able to keep his eyes open for more than sixty seconds. He acted like a man who hadn't slept in nights, and she wasn't alert enough to keep driving much longer. Her lids kept drooping, and more than once she actually dozed for an instant, jerking awake in a panic, not sure if she'd lost her concentration or actually lost consciousness for a fraction of a second. Shaky from her lapses, she knew a rest stop was imperative.

The motel had two available adjoining rooms. Eric woke up enough to walk into one, his silence conveying mild embarrassment. Here he was, the big-shot arranger, being checked into a motel like a senile old man. He felt eighty years old, aching from head to calves, his nose totally stopped up and his throat raw. Whatever fantasies he'd had about Brenda didn't involve her clucking around him with pills and syrups, playing

139

Florence Nightingale when all he wanted was to peel off his damp, wrinkled clothes and collapse on the bed. He swallowed two capsules she handed him and dismissed her with an impatient wave.

"Go catch your bus. I don't need mothering."

"You don't deserve it either." She watched him sink back on the bed after discarding his jacket. "Really, Eric, don't go back to sleep yet. Your cold will get worse if you sleep in sweaty clothes."

"I hardly think that's possible." He pressed the side of the pillow against his aching forehead.

"Did you cancel my autograph parties?"

"I'm dying, and you're worried about signing books."

"I don't like just not showing up."

"It doesn't bother you enough to go on with the tour?"

"No."

He sat up slowly, hands spread out beside his hips, annoyed by a giddy feeling that put the room out of focus.

"I think you need a doctor."

"Don't be silly. I've probably had this cold coming on for days. It'll break if I get some sleep. Go on with your life and leave me alone." He sank back, feeling as if he'd just made a long, long speech.

"Didn't your mother teach you not to put your shoes on the bed?"

"She probably did." He found himself wanting to look at her in spite of his swollen, itchy eyes, opening them cautiously to see her perched at the foot of the bed working on his laces.

"Leave my shoes alone!" he rasped, coughing from the outburst, really too weary to prevent her from sliding off his heavy black leather wing tips.

"You're being a baby." Her voice was too gentle to give her words much bite.

140

She didn't mind peeling off his socks, touching the hard knobs on his ankles, caressing the tops of his feet. She blew away a bit of dark lint that clung to his pale, veined skin.

"No tickling," he groaned.

"I didn't do it intentionally. Do you have pajamas?"

"No." How could part of him still want her when most of his body ached like a hollow tooth?

"Well, you must have something dry. I'm going to look in your suitcase."

"Check my pockets too while you're at it."

"You're too sick to be sarcastic, and I know why you're yelling at me."

She opened his suitcase and surveyed the contents. One side contained neatly arranged shoes, shaving kit, and a few dress shirts in commercial laundry packaging. The other was mostly dirty clothes in neatly tied bundles or plastic bags from his New York hotel.

"You're running out of clean clothes."

"Thanks for telling me. Aren't I keeping you from your homeward trek?"

She ignored his barbs.

His garment bag did supply a velour robe, its rich midnight-blue nap velvety under her hand. This and some clean shorts were the best she could find. Tossing them beside him on the bed, she went to the bathroom to refill his water glass, placing it on the bedside table.

"I'm going for some ice while you undress."

His mumble at least told her he was still awake.

A vending machine yielded a package of vanilla and cream cookies, one of cheese crackers with peanut butter, a bag of cheese puffs, a chocolate bar, and some lemon drops—a lousy lunch but she was starving. She'd order from room service for Eric if he wanted it. Securing two colas and a bucket of ice, she went back, entering through her door and knocking on the unlocked one

141

between their rooms before opening it. Eric was deep in sleep, still wearing his gray trousers and a wet white shirt, only his tie discarded on the floor beside the bed. His face looked terrible, pale and damp, and he stirred when she whispered his name, fumbling for a blanket.

"I'm freezing."

"I knew you'd get a chill. Fevers do that."

"No one likes a know-it-all." He attempted a grin but didn't pull it off.

She took his untouched water glass to the sink, replacing the water and adding ice cubes, really worried for the first time. He looked wretched.

Sitting beside him, she quickly unbuttoned his shirt, not wanting to touch him, fighting the exquisite pleasure it gave her to feel even the slight brush of his chest hair on her fingers. He cooperated in shedding the shirt, securing his robe around him, wrapping his arms across his front in a futile attempt to stop shivering.

"How long have you felt this coming on?"

"A day or two, I suppose. I've been too preoccupied to notice."

"Your business, I suppose."

"My business, my foot!" He fingered her cheek, warmer than his fingers and soft like a baby's, like his daughter's had been when she was a toddler, but there was nothing childlike about the small, shapely woman beside him. How far would she go to care for him in his hour of need? He wasn't too sick not to test her. "You're good at this bedside-care routine."

"You really should get out of the rest of your clothes, then I'll pile on some blankets from both rooms until you get over your chills."

Sinking back, he pretended to ignore her, closing his eyes because they didn't want to stay open anyway and clenching his teeth against the shivers.

"Is there a box of tissues in the bathroom?"

142

"Yes, I'll get it. You undress."

He didn't, and she gave him plenty of time to do so, removing the box from a metal receptacle set into the wall and washing her face before returning to his side.

"You want me to take your pants off?"

"Do you dare?" He had a hard time issuing his mock challenge without revealing a smirk. The chattering of his teeth helped.

"Really!" Her tone said he was certainly being a baby.

She managed to undo his belt and zipper with quick efficiency, pulling off his suit pants with more effort. "Now dry shorts."

She held them in front of him, but he refused to open his eyes, feeling but not seeing the covers she threw over his lower half. "Change or I'm leaving for the bus station this instant. I don't for one moment believe you're *that* sick."

"One of your heroines would rub my body with alcohol."

"I'm not anyone's heroine! And I don't have any rubbing alcohol."

"Don't shout."

"I am not shouting," she whispered. "Shall I order something to eat or would you like to sleep?"

He made a rather feeble attempt to pull her down into his arms, feeling too sick to mind her resistance, only wanting to know that she'd be there when he felt better.

"If I go to sleep, you won't leave?"

She was crazy to stay. He might feel lousy, but he wasn't hovering at death's door. When he recouped a bit, they'd have the arguments and good-byes to do all over again.

"No, I'll just eat some junk food and nap a bit next door."

"I'm shaking with cold." He sneezed violently, feeling as appealing as a skid-row bum. "Can't you keep me warm?"

"I'll get more blankets."

Leaving the connecting door open, she tried to relax on one of the two beds in her room. They had four double beds available between them, and all either wanted was to share one together. It would be so easy to snuggle beside him, warming him with her body heat, showing him the love that was swelling her heart and torturing her mind. Would it be so terrible if they lay side by side, legs entangled, hands comforting, perhaps later celebrating their closeness? The worst she could get was a cold; her doctor had kept her on a low-dosage birth-control pill for health reasons since her divorce. Her immunity to common germs was astonishing; it'd been years since she'd had even a sniffle.

Still wearing her skirt and blouse, she crept into his room, her legs bare and her feet in satin mules. His forehead was beaded with perspiration, and even asleep he looked miserable. Dampening a cloth with warm water, she gently wiped his face, then patted it with a dry towel, feeling guilty because she so badly wanted him to be awake.

When she turned to leave, his hand captured hers, tossing aside the towel and cloth, pulling her closer.

"Lie by me," he begged without opening his eyes.

"I'm sorry if I woke you."

"I'm not."

Impulsively she brushed his dry lips with hers, pulling back quickly but not escaping the hands he placed on her shoulders.

"I don't want you to get my cold." He did open his eyes now.

"I never get colds."

144

"I do. Twice a year like clockwork. My winter cold is just late this year."

"You have it now. Was it a cold, wet spring in Minnesota?"

"No, it was cold in New York."

He slid his hands to her waist. "Take off your skirt and crawl under the covers if you're not afraid of catching my cold."

"It's not your cold I'm afraid of."

"You don't really think I'd hurt you?" The misery in his voice had little to do with his illness.

"Not the way you mean!"

"How then?" He felt too exhausted to reach for her when she slipped away.

"I just don't like temporary relationships, Eric."

He closed his eyes and she regretted her words with a deep pain. There was no possibility that Eric wanted more than a few nights of fun; his look of weary resignation confirmed what she already knew.

"Sleep some more now," she managed to choke out with constricted throat muscles, leaving so quickly she didn't hear the throaty whisper that followed her.

She hadn't heard him, and maybe it was best. The words had slipped out; tomorrow he would have regretted them and not known how to take them back. He didn't tell women he loved them just to get them to bed.

CHAPTER EIGHT

His bed was surrounded by darkness, but beyond the open door he could see the eerie glow of a television set in Brenda's otherwise unlit room. Fumbling a little, he found his watch on the night stand: nearly 1 A.M. Had sleeping done his cold any good? He took a quick inventory of his pains, finding he still felt miserable but at least his acute headache had subsided.

Emerging from under a stack of blankets, he felt weak, not surprising since his last good meal had been their picnic lunch. A cautious glance into Brenda's room showed her sound asleep, propped up on pillows, facing the TV. Failing to stifle a deep cough that hurt his chest, he moved toward the bathroom, wanting a cold drink of water and a warm shower.

Cleaner, with a towel secured around his waist and another draped over his shoulders, he silently approached her bed, studying her through watery, aching eyes as she slept. Her breathing was soft and regular, making him regret the snoring he must have produced with his stuffy nose, and her skin seemed translucent in the light of the television set. She was easily the most beautiful woman he'd ever known, but he couldn't categorize her appeal. She wasn't mysterious like Garbo or regal like Leigh or vulnerably sexy like Monroe. She was just Brenda, glowing, vibrant, elusive, lovely. Not even a major cold could deaden the knife-sharp edge of his desire, and he wondered where this heady infatuation was going to lead him.

A cart with two metal-domed plates was sitting near the door; she'd ordered dinner for him, but failed to wake him to eat it. Or maybe she'd tried but the pills had made him too groggy to remember. There might still be something edible, but he stood mesmerized by the delicate face framed by a white pillow slip. He moved closer, wanting only to look at her, but a spasm deep in his chest made him cough, rousing her to semiwakefulness.

"Eric." She stared at him with sleepy concern. "You'll freeze walking around in a towel."

"Towels." The one around his waist was cold and clammy.

"Come here."

He was afraid to trust his ears, but when he crawled in on the far side of her bed, she didn't protest. The two towels made a sodden pile on the thick-napped carpeting.

Her arm across his chest was soft and warm, and her legs pressed against his side, silky smooth and very still. Afraid to break the spell by moving or speaking, he let his body go limp, basking in the soft whisper of her breath against his shoulder and the tender caress of her hand on his torso.

"Still no alcohol for a rubdown," she murmured.

"Hold me."

"Yes."

He turned his head away, hating the harsh cough that kept him from covering her mouth with his.

147

"You slept so long. I was worried." She stroked his biceps, concern etched on her face.

"It helped, I feel a little better."

He felt her hands slide to his chest and make lazy circles on his torso, soothing and warm. Covering her fingers with his colder ones, he tortured himself with visions of making love to her. The moment was precious, but he was too sick to do more than wonder at the magic of her presence. Her leg stirred against his, a small, warm foot creeping up to nestle by his, the smooth nails curling against the thin skin below his ankle.

Pulling the covers higher, she covered her own cheek, hiding it from his downcast eyes, sighing into the fine hairs over his rib cage.

"Is my head heavy?" she asked softly.

"It feels wonderful." His eyes were watering, one drop escaping to dampen the crease beside his eye.

"Are you hungry?"

"Only thirsty. I just had several glasses of water."

"There's a sandwich . . ."

"No, thank you." He touched her lips to silence her.

The television played on, a jumble of reds and blues, one of those unfortunate color productions that had deteriorated, losing the yellows and greens.

Drowsy with contentment, he knew they wouldn't make love that night, but something fragile and precious was happening between them. He didn't understand it, but he knew rushing her would be a sacrilege, like destroying a glass urn fire-blown in antiquity.

The sigh came from her heart, and again she stirred against his side, feeling closer than she'd ever felt to anyone. His skin was dry under her cheek, filling her nostrils with soapy freshness. Visions of everything that could happen between a man and a woman played through her mind, deepening the enveloping sensation

148

of oneness. At this moment just loving him was happiness.

Turning on his side away from her, he slept. She pressed her breasts to his back, making a lap with her legs to fit the firm swell of his buttocks. Electronic snow blanketed the bed in whitish light, but she couldn't bring herself to abandon him to turn off the television. When coughs racked him, as they frequently did, she whispered comfort to the back of his shoulder and held him even closer. She loved Eric Sheffield.

He awoke missing her but was reassured by the din of the shower, making him hope she'd come back to him still moist, her hair in damp ringlets, her skin rosy from toweling. Remembering the way they'd slept, locked in each other's arms, he ached for her return and questioned his own virility. To have her so close and so willing and do nothing must mean he was sicker than he thought!

He wanted to shave, brush his teeth, and swallow some cold pills to clear his miserably blocked sinuses, but he was afraid to be gone when she finished her shower. They had to be together to affirm last night and consummate their newfound closeness. Ill or not, his need for her was growing out of control. His arms ached to hold her again, and his groin felt like bursting.

"Oh, you're awake."

She was wearing a neat little cotton-blend dress, blue with a white collar. He liked the violet dress much better, but wished she hadn't dressed at all.

"Good morning." Why did he feel so self-conscious? It was no secret that he wanted her.

"You must be starved. I can't remember when you last ate a full meal." She was gathering her possessions, stowing them neatly in her suitcase.

"The picnic."

"Yes, the picnic."

He shouldn't have reminded her of it. She banged the case shut and secured the clasp with single-minded determination.

"Shall we go to breakfast?" she asked, avoiding his steady gaze.

"Sit here for a minute first." He patted the narrow strip between his hip and the edge of the bed.

"No, I don't think so, Eric. Are you feeling better?"

"That's not important!" Feeling so out of sorts made him impatient. "About last night . . ."

"You were wandering around in a wet towel. I wanted you to get warm and dry, that's all."

"Is that all?" He remembered her fingers tracing the contours of his chest. "It was more than that for me."

Her stare made him uncomfortable. Did she think he was lying?

"Was it?"

"Please." He reached out his hand, wanting to clasp her small, firm fingers.

"You really should get dressed and come to breakfast."

His patience exhausted, he threw back the covers and sat on the edge of the bed feeling irrationally guilty when she averted her eyes from his nakedness.

"It's cool in here. You seem determined to get pneumonia."

"No." He came up behind her, locking her against his bare torso and thighs, exercising all his self-control not to tear off her dress and bask in her enticing flesh. "I need you, Brenda."

"I'm here." Her voice was a strained whisper.

"Stay here."

"I'll finish the tour."

He'd practically forgotten about the tour. "It's not that important."

"Yes, it is. I agreed to go, and everything's arranged.

150

We've canceled too many appearances already. Are you well enough to go to this afternoon's?"

He didn't feel up to coping with this businesslike Brenda, ready to do her duty in a no-nonsense way.

"Order some breakfast while I shower and shave. "We'll leave as soon as I'm dressed."

Eric wanted her; he might even need her, but every minute she spent with him would increase her pain when they parted. She wanted to be courted, wooed, and won. The uncertainty in their relationship wore on her nerves. Lying with him last night, tenderness drawing them closer and closer, she'd silently yearned for some word about his feelings, knowing she was ripe to believe the most blatant lie, if he'd only pretend he loved her. But Eric didn't lie; he might be infatuated, but he was used to getting what he wanted without offering commitment.

"How long do your colds last?" she asked conversationally as they were putting the luggage in the car.

"A few days, but I've never had a chest cold this bad."

"I'll drive if you like."

"Maybe that would be better. Those cold pills make me sleepy. If you don't want to finish the tour, we can cancel," he said.

"No, I really am grateful for the opportunity. Everything you said about it is true. Anyway, I like meeting readers, and it's only the public speaking . . ."

The intensity of his stare made her lose her train of thought. Anyway, she couldn't tell him the truth: that she'd fallen in love with him and wanted to spend every possible moment with him in spite of the pain of not being loved in return.

"There's a highway sign up ahead," he said.

"You should buy some ointment for your nose. This isn't the season for Rudolph."

151

"Stay in a room with me tonight." Not a very eloquent proposition, he thought unhappily, but they'd had so little time to sort out their feelings.

She wanted to say yes but didn't. "I don't think I can. You did agree—separate rooms."

He wanted to take her in his arms and make her change her mind, but the achy stuffiness of his head restrained him. She was probably being polite when she said she never caught colds.

152

CHAPTER NINE

The tour was successful; crowds grew in size as publicity followed her appearances. Efficient managers in Indiana and Illinois arranged for several radio interviews and a spot on a local TV talk show, and Brenda learned that interview tapes were edited, cutting out hesitations and mumbles. She saw herself on a delayed broadcast, wondering if the remade, edited version of herself was the one that attracted Eric. What did he think of the real Brenda Storm, the woman with a parakeet, an ink-stained finger, and a dread of being conspicuous?

She didn't know if Eric's cold was gone; he took pills that made him moody and remote during the day. And if his cough bothered him at night, she was too far away from him to hear it.

Chicago was the culmination of the tour, and, thank heavens, she had a free day to rest up before the party at the Loop store. Eric arranged for a spacious ninth-floor motel room overlooking Lake Michigan. Below her window a small sandy beach attracted inner city swimmers and waders, while the concrete along the edge of Lake Michigan was pounded by the feet of joggers. Eric's room was in the same building, but she never saw it.

He treated her to a lovely dinner in a revolving top-floor restaurant, but spent the rest of his time at the store.

The rental car was parked on the motel's ramp, hers to use when she wanted to go home, but she took a cab to the Loop. The store was close enough to walk there, but not in her silver shoes; the towering spikes selected by Eric on the shopping spree weren't designed for city streets. Eric wanted a romantic-looking author; she felt like a walking valentine in the red chiffon dress she'd worn only for the photographer in New York. Low-cut in front, it left her arms and most of her back bare.

A train streaked down Wabash Avenue on the elevated tracks as the cab stopped in front of the store. Why couldn't Chicago bury its streetcars like any sensible city, instead of clogging the Loop with steel supports for the overhead line? She could never see this street without imagining the elevated bridge collapsing or a train falling off. Was there a name for this kind of phobia? Railaphobia? Fear of being hit on the head by a commuter car?

Don't kid yourself, she thought in near panic. It's Eric's big party, not tumbling trains, that has you scared silly. Autographs, book sales, readers, her reputation, none of these things meant anything to her unless he approved of her.

The Sheffield Bookshelf sign spanned the second story of the narrow building. Now that the tour was ending, could she look at him without revealing how she really felt?

He hadn't been this jittery since his first day in the oil fields. Then he'd expected life to be rough for a green kid who had to prove he wasn't just the boss's pampered grandson. Earning the respect of the rowdy wildcatters had been a snap compared to dealing with Brenda. Like a kid with his tongue hanging out in a candy shop, he couldn't hide how badly he wanted her.

154

Maybe bringing her here to the store was a mistake. He should have gone home with her, talked to her in private, persuaded her to—to what? He had to know what he wanted himself before he said anything to her. Whenever he heard the vibrant tone of her voice he lost his will, and smelling the light sweetness of her perfume reminded him of flower petals blown by a cool spring wind. She was stubborn, insecure, and sometimes impractical, but she was also beautiful, sexy, funny, warm, and perceptive.

"Damn!" he said aloud in his perplexity, attracting a surprised look from Ryan, a stock room assistant.

One positive thing had come out of planning the autograph session. The Loop store manager had the romance section tucked away in a back corner on the second floor. At the last tabulation nearly 20 percent of their business nationally came from different types of romantic fiction. Eric had a crew working all night, moving the romances to a prominent location on the street level where working women could spot them during their lunch hours. For some reason that escaped him, the manager had been using this choice space for foreign-language dictionaries and other slow-moving hard covers.

Besides arranging for large ads in city and suburban newspapers, he'd bought some radio spots and personally invited the members of a romance writers club to attend. A table with a huge bouquet of red roses and white carnations was set up across from the cardboard cutout of Brenda, with Ryan assigned to restock books and assist the author in any possible way. A second table was provided to serve little cups of punch and fancy tea cookies while people waited to meet her. This was one autograph session that was going to be a real party, climaxed by television coverage by a Chicago station.

He went back to the office, pretended to study a computer printout on the desk, and returned to the front just as she was coming through the door.

Seeing her was like a blow to his solar plexus. He didn't want her to look that sexy for anyone but him!

"Hello." His throat felt tight, and he was afraid to let his eyes stray to the creamy V between her breasts.

Her smile was all the greeting he needed.

"This is Ryan Douglas," he said. The kid zeroed in on her like a bird dog with a pheasant, and Eric had to overcome an impulse to boot him out instead of introducing him. "He'll keep the table stocked with books and get anything you need."

"It's a pleasure meeting you, Ryan." She clasped his thick hand and smiled warmly.

Eric was sure he was turning into a lunatic, jealous of a nineteen-year-old boy.

"Back here, Brenda." He tried for casual but his words came out brusque. Where was the famous Sheffield finesse?

Shutting the office door, he gestured at the couch, noticing for the first time a crack on the leather-upholstered armrest, then perched on the edge of his desk. From this angle he could get a glimpse of the bare swell of her breasts nestled under the red bodice of her dress. He ached to take her in his arms, not wanting to share her with anyone that afternoon. They'd gone back to separate rooms without talking about it, and his cold had nothing to do with the caution he felt about approaching her again. He wasn't at all sure what he was getting into.

Once launched, his plans turned into an author's dream party that kept Ryan running to replenish the dwindling stacks of her books. Brenda found herself enjoying, even loving, the attention, too caught up in the excitement to freeze when the TV interviewer asked questions. A few times she caught a glimpse of Eric on the fringe of the crowd, but he didn't approach her.

The afternoon was wonderful. No writer could ask for kinder, more enthusiastic readers. Eric had outdone himself in arranging publicity, but under her professional delight was one growing doubt: Had the whole affair been arranged just to stimulate business in a store with sluggish sales? The smiling cardboard image of her own face mocked her from across the aisle, and she welcomed another book buyer with a gaiety that masked her growing unease.

So many fans came that the store didn't close at 5:00 as it usually did on Saturdays. When the door was finally locked and the last romance reader gone, the store personnel hastened through their closing routine, checking out the cash, whisking away the remains of the refreshments, and wrapping the flowers in florist paper to present them to Brenda. She felt as if she should help, gathering some stray cups and napkins left on a bargain-book table, when Eric came to her side.

"This really messed up your store," she said, "but it was great, really tremendous. Thank you, Eric, very much."

"We sold a lot of your books."

"Well, that's the important thing, isn't it?"

Approval glowed on his face, but was it for her or the huge number of sales?

"They loved you." He stood very close.

"It was wonderful, but I should be going."

"Going?"

"Home. To Charlotte. I had my luggage put in the car, so all I have to do is go back to the motel parking ramp and leave."

"Stay tonight." His voice was urgent.

"I've given up my room."

"Stay in mine."

157

"Eric, I don't know . . ."

She felt unaccountably cold; maybe the air conditioning had been running while the store was crowded with people.

"At least have dinner with me."

"I'm a little nervous about driving all the way home after dark."

"Summer's nearly here. The days are getting longer."

"Not that long. It's a tedious drive."

"Please." His tongue felt swollen. "At least have a drink with me. I have a bottle of wine in the office to celebrate."

"A few sips, maybe. I am driving." Her laugh was pretty feeble, and she already felt intoxicated.

They were the only ones left in the store, and she followed him down a narrow corridor to the office. The room was windowless but brightly lit by overhead neons that made his face look pale. She anticipated his kiss before he moved. Backing up until the edge of the desk was pressing against her bottom, she nervously moistened her lips, afraid her feelings would race out of control.

"Brenda."

Her plain name sounded like an incantation, and he hesitated for such a long moment she was sure the kiss would never come. When he bent his head, his lips only brushed her forehead.

A kiss on the forehead was hardly threatening, but she was living dangerously, flirting with the idea of staying the night with Eric. She wanted to be with him. There wasn't one good reason why she should refuse the man she loved. Maybe she'd subconsciously decided to accept any offer he made even before checking out of the motel at noon. The risk of being hurt was beginning to seem trivial compared to the possibility of never seeing him again.

"You're lovely in that dress."

"Thank you. I hope I looked romantic enough." Her shoulders quivered just a little.

"More than enough. I wish you'd wear it just for me. It's probably the most beautiful dress I've ever seen, with you in it," he said softly.

"You're exaggerating." She hoped he wasn't.

"No. There are billions of words on the shelves out there, but I can't seem to find the ones I need."

She locked her fingers together, more agitated than she'd been in front of the TV camera. Surely the admiration on his face was a kind of self-congratulation. He'd taken a shy scribbler from southern Illinois and changed her into a romantic media personality. He wouldn't be the first man to be infatuated with his own creation.

She needed to say something to gain time. "I'm using New Hampshire as the setting for one of my new books. I should see if you have a good New England travel guide in the store."

What a ninny she was, deliberately switching to a harmless subject! She knew it would be better to leave for home right away as she'd planned.

"I'm sure we must. Do you want to look?" He was getting in too deep; the real world of books would settle him down. "They're on the second floor. Let's go see."

"I don't want to put you to a lot of trouble. The store's dark."

"Lights can be turned on."

Lightly touching her arm, he guided her into the store, deserted now with low-watt lights more eerie than comforting. He led the way to the unmoving escalator, taking her hand so the spike heels wouldn't trip her on the ridged steps. The second floor was even darker, but he flipped a wall switch, and it was illuminated.

"How many floors have books for sale?"

"All three."

"Can I see the top one?"

"Sure, why not?" He didn't care what they did as long as he could bask in her presence like a dehydrated man soaking up water.

The third floor had a lower ceiling and row after row of tables holding books. Any other time she would have browsed like the book fanatic she was, reading nearly every title and examining dozens of blurbs until she piled up a stack for her already huge library. Tonight she was aware only of his hand resting on her waist. He was wearing a suit the color of wet sand with a tie that reminded her of butterscotch taffy, looking so handsome he brought a catch to her throat.

"The travel books are one floor down," he said.

She let him guide her, one arm around her shoulders. At the bottom of the steps he took her in his arms, his hands resting on the bare skin of her back.

"What book was it you wanted?" His chin brushed her hair, and his hands moved slowly lower.

She couldn't remember.

He covered her mouth with his, the gentle pressure deepening as her lips came alive, returning his kiss with a kind of desperation. His tongue flicked against the fleshy inside of her upper lip, darting and teasing, rousing her as she clutched at his shoulders. She felt the sinewy muscles under the smooth material of his jacket and ran her hands down his arms.

Backing her slowly toward a long table of hardcover books arranged in piles, he clasped her waist and lifted her, seating her on a stack of oversize art books, reclaiming her mouth with a fervor that took away her breath. His tongue played with hers, hiding, pushing, then overpowering, while his hands warmed the skin of her back.

Sliding forward on the insecure perch, she hung in his

160

arms, clinging to his neck to maintain her precarious balance, expecting books to slide out from under her at any second. Easing her backward, he didn't seem to notice the thud when some did fall off on the other side of the table. He released her mouth and smiled gently, his face transformed by what he felt for her. So slowly that it didn't occur to her to stop him, he ran his hand over her knee and along her inner thigh, then fingered the taut nylon over her crotch until she boiled. She groped for a firmer handhold among the stacks of books and another pile fell to the floor with a noisy clatter.

"I'm ruining your display." She gasped as his hands got bolder.

Without his body as a brace she'd tumble to the floor. When he traced the crease where her leg and torso were joined, she grabbed for support and made a jumbled mess of the books to her left.

"Never mind them," he said, wedging his fingers under her thighs until she was almost sitting on his hands.

"The book. I was going to look for the book." She wiggled until her toes touched the carpeted floor, but his hands stayed with her, kneading her buttocks, locking her against him.

"What book was that?" He pressed warm lips to the hollow of her neck and ran his hands over the front of her dress.

Ducking under his arm, she hurried out of reach and feigned interest in the wall shelves to her right, running sightless eyes over neat rows of books.

"Auto mechanics. I didn't know you did your own repairs," he teased, coming up behind her.

"You have every imaginable topic here." Her voice sounded hollow, and her breath was bubbling out in a very peculiar way.

"How to do everything—even make love." He

stroked her arm, appreciating the well-proportioned slimness.

"I think I see something," she said.

She yanked free, skirted several tables, and stopped by a ladder that slid along the wall for easier shelf stocking. Without noticing what the books were behind it, she climbed up, hanging on with both hands while her instep bit into a narrow rung.

"Can I help you?" His head was level with her knees.

The books at eye level had something to do with oriental culture, but the hand on the back of her calf was bent on a universal pleasure, caressing the nylon of her hose as she tightened her whole body against his assault.

"Brenda."

"What?" She was frozen on the ladder.

"Come down."

It was an order, but she was through being intimidated. There was only one good reason for going into his arms: she wanted to be there more than anything in the world.

"You're being bossy," she said.

"Only because I'm desperate. I want you, darling."

She lowered one foot, half turning toward him, aware of how easy it would be for him to lift her off.

"Want me? My heroes never say that!" She went one step lower.

"I want to be your lover, not one of your heroes."

She fell the rest of the way into his arms, clinging to his neck when he scooped her against his hard chest.

Without speaking, he carried her down the escalator, only a low sigh betraying the pleasure he felt when her lips nibbled at the hollow of his neck and her fingers traced the shape of his ear. Inside the door of his office he had a momentary vision of the spacious bed in his motel room, but it was far away and he'd waited too long. He lowered her until her feet touched the floor, flicked out the overhead lights, and found the switch of the desk lamp.

Kicking off her shoes, she stood on the tops of his feet, gaining the few inches needed to press her cheek against his, circling his back with her arms and melting against his hard body.

"Hold me," she murmured unnecessarily, feeling the flicker of his lashes on her eyelids when he bent to cover her mouth with his.

Her tongue darted impulsively against his teeth, then explored the hollows of his cheeks and the roof of his mouth, swelling to caress his softly grained tongue. She could hear her own heart beating like a drum, and she shuddered with excitement.

The red dress drove him wild, soft and yielding but defying his best efforts to cast it aside. He fondled her breasts, feeling taut nipples under the cloth, but the material couldn't be mastered without ripping it. Who'd suspect such flimsy armor would be so resistant? He fumbled with the cloth on her shoulders but couldn't slide it over her smooth upper arms.

Reaching for him, she slowly unbuttoned his shirt button by button, stopping to kiss the skin she exposed, feeling the thundering beat of his heart, not stopping when the shirt was a pile at their feet but timidly loosening his trousers, sliding down the zipper and pushing the smooth-textured pants over his hip bones, slipping off his other garments until he stood naked before her, his body betraying him, his hands too shaky to tackle the intricacies of her dress.

Her eyes never turned aside, and her faint smile was that of a temptress. Her fingers flitted across his chest, so light they felt like butterfly wings beating against his torso, teasing his nipples with no more pressure than the scurrying of an ant's feet.

163

He sucked in air, stunned by the erotic effect of her feathery touch, sure that she was either a witch or the most incredible woman he'd ever known. He forced himself to be absolutely still as her fingers crept lower, tormenting his navel and combing his thickening hair, making his thighs quiver.

"Let me see you." His voice sounded miles away.

When she slid down a zipper concealed on the side of the dress, he didn't need any more help.

Her breasts, freed from constraining cloth, were warm and heavy in his hands, fuller than her delicate bone structure suggested, so soft he was afraid of hurting them, so desirable he was giddy. He bent to kiss her then, feeling her hands massaging the expanse of his back. This eager, passionate woman was driving him to distraction, more than meeting him halfway, delighting in him. He wanted to whoop with joy and lose himself in desire. She was even more woman than her books had suggested. Someday he'd tell her the truth: he'd read every one, entertained by her imagery and imagination. It seemed as if he'd been waiting for her all his life.

He led her to the couch, the leather cool and sticky under her back, but she didn't even notice the discomfort. Loving and wanting him, she stroked his body with her tongue and fingers, wrapping her legs around his hips in invitation. He was caressing her thighs, so instinctively kind that her heart ached with tenderness. He crooned and called her darling, telling her she was sweet and beautiful and fantastic, repetition making a melodic buzz in her ears. She'd never tell him to stop humming again.

Seemingly incapable of crudeness or roughness, he made love with intense control, making her pores sing and her flesh yearn for him. Her nostrils were filled with his musk, the incense of love, and exertion only made

164

his flesh more sensual to her. Lithe and compact, his body had reserves of strength that helped him coax the last tremor of satisfaction from her quivering body.

For a long time they lay, legs and arms entwined, her cheek moist against his chest, savoring and remembering, too euphoric to feel cramped or uncomfortable on the couch. He wiggled until his body was stretched out under her, relaxed and inviting, dark hairs clinging to his torso in a damp mat. Nipping at his grinning lips, she willed their time together to go on and on and on.

Love made her powerful, expanding her potential and making her feel in control of her destiny. Nothing she'd ever imagined prepared her for the raw explosion of feeling she experienced with Eric. He was no sluggish lover who spent his passion and left her aching. The trance that followed their lovemaking was nothing like sleep; their senses were acute, and the joy of touching didn't pall. When, much later, they did doze, it was from physical exhaustion.

Awaking slowly, she moved with extreme care, untangling her leg from between his, being careful not to wake him. When he stirred and mumbled, she froze, but he only settled his bottom more comfortably against the back of the couch and covered his eyes with his arm.

Her body felt logy and satisfied, but disappointment was making her forget their fantastic physical union. Never once, not even in the heat of passion, had Eric said he loved her. They'd enjoyed each other—immensely, if she was honest with herself—but the pleasure was everything for him.

She wasn't sorry for making love. Her senses were still singing. The evening had been magic, and never again would her heroines be submissive. They'd be total partners in expressing physical love. For this heightened awareness of what lovemaking could be, she'd always thank Eric, but gathering insight and experience meant very little besides knowing her love was not returned. The flip side of love was pain. She couldn't bear to stay near him hoping for crumbs of affection when she wanted to share his whole life.

She left him sleeping on the couch.

CHAPTER TEN

Everything was as she'd left it. The blue-flowered mug sitting on her drainboard had been there for weeks, but she felt as if her trip had lasted years. Walking through the house, she pushed a chair up to the kitchen table, fluffed a needlepoint pillow her mother had made from a kit, and carried a drooping bouquet of spring flowers, forgotten in her rush to leave for the romance conference, to the garbage disposal, grinding up their wilted beauty in a rush of water. The stems smelled horribly of decay, and she wanted to cry because so many wonderful things in life faded so quickly. Tears came to her eyes as she dried her hands on a dish towel embroidered with a windmill.

He could call if he wanted to see her again. Finally running out of tears, she tried to convince herself he would call. She even checked both phones, in the kitchen and her office, to make sure they were working.

Three days passed, and she gave up listening for the phone. He wasn't going to call.

Open drapes let hazy yellow light into the long bedroom that occupied the entire second level of her story-and-a-half house. The pale oak paneling took on a honey hue and dust motes danced in the sunlight. She sat up slowly, not sure whether she'd slept minutes or hours. Her pillowcase still felt damp from another long, bitter cry, and getting up seemed like more effort than it was worth.

Her injured pride told her that Eric Sheffield had barged into her life, shanghaied her into a promotional tour because he wanted to sleep with her, and succeeded in seducing her. Her heart told her other things: life without him was colorless and barren. She wasn't very good at lying to herself; the fling she'd once wanted to avoid had brought her to a miserable state.

Forcing down some rye toast and tea, she admitted that what had happened in Eric's office had nothing to do with seduction. Her love had been a gift offered with full awareness of the consequences. She'd wanted him with every ounce of desire in her, responding to him with an assertiveness that still made her marvel. For better or worse, her life had changed. She couldn't possibly hide in her little house and wait for the good things to come to her. The right man wasn't going to fall from the sky onto her lap.

The right man was Eric, only he didn't know it.

Her office was a comforting clutter of books and manuscripts. Typed and longhand copies lay in different-colored boxes that identified their state of readiness. Losing herself in her work had had a healing benefit before; it would again. Assigning herself the task of reviewing what was done, she reread finished chapters, then went on to her scrawling longhand pages. After an hour she didn't remember a word. The scenes of her latest book ran hazily through her mind, leaving only a useless residue.

Sitting with her lap desk and trying to begin the next chapter, she wasn't any more successful. Matt, her hero, couldn't communicate with the woman he loved, and the few lines of dialogue she put on paper were as stilted as a nineteenth-century farce.

Pacing, consuming half a jar of strawberry jam on crackers, and carrying her work to the breezeway all failed to nudge her brain into action. For the first time in her writing career she had a genuine writer's block. Words evaded her, and only mental images of Eric were shooting through her mind: Eric smiling, Eric with his face softened by passion, Eric stretching his arms above his head, his body tufted with patches of dark, silky hair, Eric taking her in his arms. . . .

Abandoning the lap desk and box of paper on the lounger, she headed for her garden. When all else fails, try manual labor, she thought.

Hours later her legs were stiff from stooping, her hands were encrusted with rich black dirt, and her lavender knit top was sticking damply to her back. Tinges of sunburn were making themselves felt on the backs of her arms and legs, and she was gritty enough to deserve an hour-long soak in a tub bubbling over with foamy scented water. Instead she took a quick shower, gave fresh seed and water to her brilliant green bird, and went back to her writing.

"Shakespeare, you could write a better chapter than I can today," she said dejectedly to her caged pet.

Maybe she was totally burned out on the subject of romance. Maybe there was a future for her writing children's books.

She was never going to sleep again. Her eyes were glued open, not even blinking in the curtained darkness of her bedroom, and no position possible to the human body allowed her to relax. The room was too warm, the bed too lonely, the future too bleak. The faint hope that Eric would contact her had faded away.

Without turning on the lights, she crept down the carpeted stairs in bare feet, making her way by instinct and feel into her office, then remembering that the hopeless chapter had been abandoned on the breezeway.

A summer breeze was coming through the louvered windows, fanning her warm skin where the skimpy nightgown didn't cover it. Snapping on the overhead light, yellow to discourage insects, she sat on the red-and green-flowered cushions of the lounger, wiggling to put some cloth between her bare bottom and the plastic upholstery. Several pens rattled in the box that had once held typing paper, and she settled the lap desk on her knees and started writing.

In the morning they wouldn't remember the bolts of lightning that split the iron-gray sky. Matt knelt, his cheek on her knee, caressing the scarlet triangle of smooth cloth with one blunt but gentle finger, using his thumb as though he were tenderly parting the petals of an exquisite bloom.

The sun rose above Brenda's well-tended garden, painting the sky crimson and orange, but she gave the spectacular solar display only a fleeting glance. Her characters were coming alive under the flying point of her pen, loving each other with a sense of joy and abandonment that had been lacking in even the best of her other books. All that mattered to Matt and Sandy was a future together, and when fate conspired to rend them apart, the author shed tears. She'd never done a better night's—or day's—work.

The townspeople of Charlotte, Illinois, were just beginning to stir when Brenda crawled into bed with weary satisfaction.

Her house looked suspiciously quiet with not a window open in the front, and the morning paper was still stuck on the metal prongs of the mailbox. Her mail, several business-size envelopes and a smaller one with a pink-checkered border, was there too, and he made a bundle of the paper and letters, pushing a black-buttoned door buzzer beside the closed door. Even if she had air conditioning, wouldn't she open the house on such a pleasant morning? In fact, it was almost afternoon; his quartz watch said 11:47.

He rang again, an impatient series of blasts that should have roused a hibernating bear. Deciding to check the garage for a car, he was just turning away when the door opened.

"Good morning." He sounded gruff as he tried to conceal a totally alien feeling of shyness.

"Eric."

He awkwardly thrust the paper bundle at her as he entered, dropping it on the seat of an old-fashioned hall tree when she didn't take it.

"I woke you."

"Yes, I worked late last night. Until the sun came up."

She looked exactly as he wanted to see her, her eyes still hooded with sleep and her hair tousled in unruly ringlets. A short kimono, brilliant with reds, pinks, and purples, was tied at her waist, but her legs were bare from mid-thigh to the bottom of her feet. Barefooted, she seemed smaller and more vulnerable, but the guarded expression on her face belied her doll-like appearance.

"I'm sorry I woke you." He wasn't.

"Why did you come?"

"You believe in getting right to the point, don't you?"

"Yes."

He wandered through her small living room, seeing the kitchen beyond it. The furniture reminded him of dollhouse furnishings, warm maple with splotches of sunny gold and forest green, but the prints on the wall were too bold and sophisticated to maintain the illusion

171

of a miniature setting. He recognized one of Moss's enchanting city scenes and a fantasy landscape by an exciting new Spanish-American artist.

"I like your prints."

"They don't go with the furniture."

"No. Which came first?"

"My ex-husband liked Early American."

"I see."

"What do you see?" She ran her fingers through her hair without realizing she was doing it.

"Nothing."

Not for the first time an unpleasant suspicion rose like bile in his throat. She was standing like a sentinel at the bottom of a stairway, feet spread and digging into the pile of the carpeting.

"Tell me," he asked, "is there someone else?"

The question surprised her so much she didn't answer.

"I thought you might be living with someone," he said woodenly, imagining that she'd just come from a bed she shared with another man.

"No, there's no one." She didn't dare say, "no one else."

She'd certainly succeeded in triggering his imagination. "I wanted to see you," he said lamely.

"Oh?" She couldn't conceal her anxiety. Her future was dangling on a slender thread, and he was a polite stranger again, not taking her in his arms and kissing away her doubts. She could read the longing in his gaze, but his lips were set in a stern line and his brows were puckered.

"I was furious when I woke up alone. I went to the motel ramp to see if the car was gone."

"I should've told you I was leaving." This was true; she'd taken the cowardly course and wasn't proud of it.

"Eric . . ."

They each moved a step closer, their eyes meeting for the first time.

"I came to tell you . . ."

"The doorbell."

"Ignore it."

"In this town people know if I'm home."

Her caller certainly was persistent, ringing almost as impatiently as he had.

"Julie," Brenda said, greeting her sister.

"Don't tell me you weren't up yet." She was the early-bird sister. "Mom said you were home, but you haven't called me. I thought . . ." She stepped into the living room and saw Eric. "Oh."

"Julie, this is Eric Sheffield." She remembered her nightgown and kimono. "Of Sheffield Bookshelves."

All of her sister's liberal theories were being put to the test, and she wavered between admiration and disapproval. Her eyes flew over his short-sleeved white knit shirt and casual tan slacks, then inspected his feet, clad in brown loafers.

"Eric just came," Brenda explained. "This is my sister, Julie."

Julie flashed her a "who are you kidding?" glance and took the hand he offered.

"I'm to blame for waking Brenda," he said. "It's really nice to meet you, Julie."

Brenda was used to his devastating charm, but she was taken aback by the near-lethal dose he leveled at her sister. Both of them ignored her completely for what seemed like hours, Eric seemingly entranced by her sister's overly dramatic account of the barn burning.

"No one has barn raisings anymore," her sister went on, "but you must come out to the farm anyway. You haven't had a real country dinner until you've tried sweet corn frozen on the cob."

When she had company Julie sometimes begged some

home-frozen produce from her mother-in-law. Her own meals owed more to supermarket frozen foods than to good ol' down-home cookin'.

"Did you come for a reason, Julie?" Brenda had thought they were beyond sibling rivalry!

"Just checking on my little sister. Have you had your morning tea yet?" Julie asked, so obviously angling for an invitation to stay that Brenda wanted to thwart her.

"Yes. Are you going on to Mom's?"

"I have to stop at the store later for some yarn."

"If you go now, you can catch her before she goes to lunch. Tell her I'm busy finishing my new book, but I'll call her soon."

"I didn't know you were working."

"I worked all night."

"Then I'd better leave. I know how touchy you are when you don't get enough sleep."

"I've had plenty of sleep."

It took Eric five minutes to walk Julie to the door. She nearly twittered when he kissed her hand.

"I thought hand kissing went out with high-button shoes," Brenda said, deciding a cup of tea wasn't such a bad idea.

He was standing uncomfortably close, watching intently as she filled a cup with hot water and stuck it in the microwave.

"I have instant coffee, if you'd like some."

"Please."

"Do you want an English muffin?"

"With jam?"

"No jam." She'd finished it trying to cure her writer's block. "Cinnamon sugar."

"Even better."

She toasted several muffins, but neither of them seemed to be very hungry or very talkative.

"Your sister's charming."

174

"Usually."

"But she's had a hard life."

"Julie?" If anyone knocked aside life's obstacles with stylish élan, it was her sister.

"Competing with you. It's not fair having a younger sister as beautiful as you."

"I think I'd better go upstairs and get dressed."

Let him see the real Brenda in faded jeans and that old cotton shirt she'd rescued from her father's rummage sale to wear when she painted the garden fence. She didn't bother with makeup or a curling iron, but she took a long time making the bed and straightening her room. Why was Eric here?

The breezeway between the kitchen and garage looked invitingly cool; he wasn't leaving until things were settled between them. The lounger looked like a comfortable place to wait. He just didn't know how to approach her.

A typing-paper box was in his way, so he picked it up, intending to set it aside. Realizing what it was, he changed his mind. It was a manuscript, maybe the one that had kept her working through the night.

He read rapidly, occasionally skipping over a hard-to-read word scrawled in her fast-flowing script, but enthralled by the job she'd done with her characters. They were real people with conflicts that weren't easy to resolve.

He read:

Matt slowly turned to look at her, closer to crying than he'd been since early childhood.

"All I've ever wanted is to love you."

"But you've never said you love me."

"I do."

He opened his arms to receive her trembling form, pressing her close, feeling the heaving of her

175

breasts, kissing her forehead and silently imploring her to stop sobbing.

"I love you, darling, more than life."

Without knowing what came before, Eric was still oddly touched. "I love you." They were simple little words full of hidden meaning and pitfalls. He'd never said them to anyone since his divorce. A woman could read so much into those three words: faithfulness, commitment, eternal togetherness. Why say something so fraught with misinterpretations and misunderstandings?

Why say "I love you" unless you meant it?

"Oh, you're reading my chapter."

She wasn't pleased. There was something too personal and revealing about rough copy. It needed the laborious polishing she gave all her work before anyone read it.

"It's very good," he said. "Maybe the best you've done."

"You've only read one of my books."

"No, I've read all the ones I could find."

"When?"

"Recently. This is good stuff."

He shuffled the pages and started reading aloud:

The porch swing creaked, the chains unoiled for many seasons, but he kept it moving with one foot, the sound grating on his nerves but distracting him from thoughts too volatile to handle. Across the way, the big house was dark. . . .

"I know what it says, Eric. Please don't read it to me!"

"You shouldn't be embarrassed by good prose."

"I'm embarrassed because I know what comes next."

"Ah, yes, he's the hired man and she's the landowner's daughter. But she's alone tonight, and he's . . ."

"Never mind!"

Her door was open just a crack, and he could see the four-poster bed, the comforter pushed aside. She stirred under the sheet, then slowly sat, sensing rather than hearing him.

"Pa told me to latch the door."

"You didn't."

"No."

The sheet slipped to her waist, revealing the swelling buds of her breasts.

Eric's voice gave the scene magical properties, but she couldn't bear to hear more.

"Brenda!"

She slipped past him, running to the garden so cozily fenced by head-high boards. It was her refuge and delight, neat rows of vegetables, some not even sprouting yet, the seed envelopes stuck into the ground with sticks. She always grew far more than she could use, and in a town where gardening was the favorite outdoor sport, it was sometimes hard to make good use of all her produce. Yet every year she planted more, loving ripe tomatoes hanging on branches that seemed too slender, lacy-topped carrots, and even the fat orange pumpkins that provided enough pulp to make pumpkin bread for the whole town. Julie had the hungry husband, and she had the full freezer, the fruit of her own efforts.

He followed, of course, carefully walking in what he thought were paths between the planted rows.

"Do you take care of all this yourself?"

"Yes."

"You're good at taking care of things, aren't you?"

"What do you mean?"

177

"You don't let any brambles get in your path."

"You're purposely being obscure."

"Maybe. I love you, Brenda."

She kept her face averted. "You think that's what I want to hear."

"Isn't it?"

"Not if my book gave you the idea!"

"It's a beautiful book."

"It's make-believe, Eric!"

"This isn't." He took her in his arms, kissing her as he'd been dying to do since she first opened her door.

"No." The protest came from deep in her throat, and he released her, watching her run toward the house.

If she locked the door against him, it would be the end of his hopes. He walked with painful slowness, feeling double his years. Even with the metal handle under his hand, he was afraid to try it. When the door slid open with well-lubricated ease, a loud sigh escaped from his constricted chest.

He found her in the office, motionless in front of an uncovered typewriter.

"When a man says he loves you, it's not polite to run for cover."

"Polite?" Her mind seemed miles away. "Polite is for strangers."

He rested his hands lightly on her shoulders, smiling at the frumpy shirt she'd put on for his benefit.

"I did a terrible thing," he said softly.

"What?"

"I didn't tell you sooner." He slipped his fingers under the mannish cotton collar and gently kneaded her neck and throat.

She managed a faint smile, placing a hand on top of his when he slid it under the first button of her shirt.

"I do love you," he said.

She was melting on her old leather-covered typing

chair, wanting him so much she felt possessed. With eyes downcast and hands locked together on her lap, she felt him swivel the chair until they were facing each other. Even when he got down on his knees beside her, she couldn't look directly into his face. If she read any doubt or deception in his eyes, it would be the end of her existence.

"Don't say anything you don't mean," she begged.

"I haven't."

He separated her hands, spreading apart the little finger on one, gently kissing and flicking his tongue in the space beside it, doing the same with the other fingers, then pressing his lips to the pale, veined skin of her wrist.

Her free hand strayed to the head bent so intently over her fingers, stroking his hair, brushing it back from his forehead. A single gray hair among the rich chestnut ones made her feel like weeping; time passed so quickly, and they needed each other so much. But her own reticence made her understand his. They weren't young enough to casually join their lives together; that was for the immature and the reckless, and they were neither.

"I love you, Brenda." The words seemed so right, so perfect, that he wanted to shout them to the heavens, his joy shadowed only by the fear that she might not feel the same for him.

After waiting so long for his declaration of love, she couldn't find the words to confess her own love. Why didn't she crush his head against her body and use all the power of speech to let him know how much she loved him? While he kissed her other hand, she was paralyzed, capable only of passively receiving his offerings.

"Brenda." He reached under the ridiculously loose shirt, resting his palm against her midriff, feeling the pounding of her heart and the warmth of smooth skin.

179

Her hands hung limply by her sides now, denying herself the tactile pleasure of touching him, her eyes closed but her mind seeing all that he did. Starting at the bottom, he slowly unbuttoned the worn shirt until the front parted, revealing her breasts, aching under a plain cotton bra. His slowness was maddening but so exciting she clenched her fists in anticipation, willing him to make love to her.

Her passive acceptance was more arousing than he could have imagined, and when he stroked her nipples, still imprisoned by the sturdy cloth, her shudder ran through his body too. Haste was unthinkable; anything but gentleness seemed unforgivable. He outlined the hard tips of her breasts with his forefingers, then held his tongue motionless between her parted lips.

Rising to his feet, he pulled her into his arms, parting her legs with his knee and holding her very still while they drank in the intoxicating closeness. Again his tongue found entry to the moist recesses of her mouth, not thrusting or darting but swelling against her tongue. Her breath tickled his nose, and her hands fluttered against his back like the wings of a baby bird. When he lifted her in his arms, she clung to his neck, bathing one chosen spot below his ear with moist little kisses. The stairway ended in her bedroom, and he let her feet slide to the floor without releasing her shoulders. With all his senses heightened, he surveyed the room with approval: paneled walls, polished floorboards with thick rose throw rugs, a quilted spread, flowery in shades of rose and pink with matching curtains, and white painted furniture trimmed in gold. The ceilings were slanted with windows at either end and no wall space for pictures, but china figurines in pastel shades wearing costumes of the eighteenth century stood on the dresser and chest. It was a wholly feminine room without silliness or frilliness. He kissed her again, slowly drinking in the sweetness of her mouth.

Both windows were open, and although the room was warm, the air was fresh.

"I love you." He was like an addict, unable to resist indulging in the words again and again.

When he dropped her droopy shirt to the floor, she sighed with pleasure but did nothing to help him. The kisses he bestowed on her throat and breasts made her tremble with longing, but still she remained passive, testing, frozen with wonder, while he freed her arms of the bra straps and her legs of the jeans.

He stopped when she was left wearing only pink panties, and much more quickly stripped off his own clothing. Turning his back, he made a fast pile of his garments on the floor, filling her with admiration for his lithe frame, strong legs, and compact, masculine buttocks. He was beautiful. She didn't even stop to consider whether this word would be out of place describing one of her heroes.

Walking first to one window and then the other, he drew the curtains. She could have told him no neighbor could see into her secluded room with the leafy maples shadowing it, but the dimness of the light heightened her passion, making it seem secretive and magical.

He rolled her panties down then, over her hips and down her thighs. Bending to free them from her feet, he gracefully arched his spine, and she leaned over him to trace the knobs of his backbone, caressing lightly freckled skin, letting her fingers slide where they would. Straightening, he smiled happily and hugged her against him, undulating his body until they swayed together in a dance without steps, his hands running up and down her back and cupping her buttocks with delightfully naughty fingers.

She thought their love would consume them as they

181

stood there. They couldn't touch each other enough, so lost in the experience that meaningless sounds erupted from their throats. Straining against him, running her nails in a feathery-light path over his shoulders and back, she forgot who and what she was, living wholly to be his.

In a final burst of self-control, he threw aside the spread, peeling the covers off to reveal the bottom sheet, and tumbled with her onto the smooth pink cotton surface.

Aroused beyond the stage of patient lovemaking, he took her as he'd never before taken a woman, quickly, urgently, almost violently, becoming so much a part of her that they had no separate existence. Her hair smelled like sunshine in his nostrils, and her skin was as warm and moist as his but infinitely sweeter. The arms and legs circling his heaving body were so strong he'd never again see her as a doll, and her teeth ground against his mouth while fulfillment rocked their universe.

Collapsing on top of her, he buried his face in her hair, knowing his weight would crush her and willing himself to release her. When he did stir, her arms and legs held him there.

"Say it again," she murmured.

Knowing what she meant, he whispered, "I love you." Suddenly he needed to hear her say the same thing more than he needed to breathe. He leaned over her on his elbows, searching her face, hoping against hope. "And you?"

"I've never known anyone like you."

"Is that all?" He rolled to her side but held her there with one arm.

"I care about you very much." Her voice was a throaty whisper.

He couldn't believe his own disappointment. How

could she make love like a siren, then casually say she "cared" about him?

Wiggling under his arm, she averted her eyes to avoid his searching appraisal of her face. Making love with him was so wonderful it hurt. If she didn't get up now it would happen again and again and again, until he was ready to go away. When would that be? Tonight? Tomorrow? The next day? Did it really matter when he left, if she had to lie alone on this bed that had once been soaked by a bittersweet flood of passion?

She tried to get away from the restraining weight of his arm, but he had no scruples about using his strength to keep her where he wanted her.

"I want to know if you love me," he said.

"Yes, I do."

"Then stay here. Let me hold you in my arms instead of holding you down." He gently kissed her pink, swollen lips, running his tongue between them but not attempting to pass the barrier of her teeth.

"Are you going to leave soon?" she asked in desperation.

"Do you really think all I want is a tussle in bed?" He felt as if he'd been slapped.

Sitting up, he pulled the sheet up to her chin, covering the moist triangle above her deliciously plump thighs and the buds of her breasts. He couldn't talk sense to a woman who could make him ache with desire just by wiggling her hips. He wanted to fill his mouth with the tang of her flesh and lose himself between the softness of her thighs, but even that wouldn't satiate him. He wanted more, so much more that he felt stymied and inadequate.

Lying on his side, making sure the sheet covered him too, he propped himself on one elbow and stared at her with pain in his eyes.

"Is the tour still a problem between us?"

"Maybe indirectly." She had nothing to lose by telling the truth now.

"My motives weren't in the least bit noble." He sighed with frustration, wishing she wasn't so guarded and wary. "I wanted you."

"The Chicago party was fantastic." She meant the autographing.

"I wasn't a very good host." He smiled at the thought of the leather couch sticking to his sweaty skin.

"Yes, you were." She knew he wasn't talking about fans or publicity.

He traced the features on her face, then parted her lips. She gave his thumb a love bite, meeting his eyes and seeing them cloud with passion again. The sheet wasn't enough to make him forget what was under it; his hand cupped one breast that was swelling against the thin covering, but she pushed it away.

"I don't want to have an affair." At last she blurted out her true feelings.

"Is that what this is?"

"Isn't it?"

His foot brushed hers, but she quickly moved away. She'd never been able to understand why his leg, hard and hairy, was so sexy.

"No, it's not! I love you! And I think you love me. You can fool your readers into thinking Matt is a fictional character, but I know better!"

Her embarrassment showed in flushed cheeks and averted eyes. She'd always insisted there were no real people in her books. Until now there never had been. It was like having her soul stripped naked to know that Eric recognized himself in Matt.

"It doesn't matter what you think. Matt is fictional."

"You're a lousy liar."

His kiss started as punishment but didn't end until they were clinging together in heated abandon.

"Not now." He moved away from her, sounding harsh because it was himself he had to restrain. He'd never wanted to make love to a woman more urgently than now. A lifetime of frenzied couplings wouldn't be enough to get her out of his system, and now that was the last thing he wanted to do.

"You have to know," he said slowly, lying flat on his back and not looking at her. "After one failure at marriage that was more my fault than my ex-wife's, I was extremely leery of trying again."

"I understand." Actually hearing him admit it made her want to cry.

"That was before I met you." He spoke slowly, still not sure he could say what had to be said.

His hand found hers and carried it to his chest, holding it against his thudding heart.

"I've changed my mind," he admitted with some lingering traces of hesitation.

"When?" She wanted to ask why but didn't, afraid to believe in something she wanted so desperately to be true.

"Maybe when a hot little number made me take three falls on the office couch."

"What an awful way to put it! I never 'made' you do anything."

"No? You made me fall in love. This morning when you opened the door, I wanted to be with you forever. Have I told you you're most beautiful when you first wake up?"

"No." Now she felt like crying for joy. She wasn't his made-over creation when she first woke up.

"I don't suppose you'd like to live with me?"

She shriveled with disappointment until she realized he was teasing.

"Here?"

185

"Establish national headquarters for Sheffield Book-shelves in Charlotte?"

"Not a good idea, huh?"

"No."

They were both staring up at the ceiling, communicating with hands locked together between them.

"We could live together awhile and get married when we feel like it," he suggested, this time sounding just a little hopeful.

"I don't think so."

"Wedding bells?"

"The bells aren't necessary."

"I won't put up with an army of bored groomsmen in monkey suits or a bunch of fluttery bridesmaids."

"That doesn't seem important anymore."

"We can just tell each other we're married. A marriage license is only a piece of paper."

"An important one."

"My darling, your chances of getting away from me with or without it are worse than the prospects of an elephant who wants to fly."

"What if there's ever someone else?"

"I once thought of turning you over my knee . . ."

"Forget that! What if you find someone else?"

"Your ex-husband did?"

"Eventually, yes, but I'm talking about us, you and me."

"Do you lie awake worrying that a tidal wave from Lake Michigan will swamp the Midwest?"

"Of course not."

"Then you'd better start, because a tidal wave is more likely than the end of my love for you. I've waited too long for you."

He had to kiss her then, a long, delightful, toe-tingling buss that left them both breathless. She snuggled

186

against him, her whole body a warm, pulsating invitation, but he wiggled aside and held her away from him.

"You're forgetting something," he said, nuzzling her knuckles and pushing her legs away with his foot.

"What?"

"Think!" He pinned both of her legs with one of his.

"Do you want to know if I'll marry you?" she asked.

"Will you?"

"I think so."

"Think so!" He rolled on top of her and bedeviled her nose with his tongue. "Think so! Do you know what it costs me to consider a ridiculous arrangement like marriage?"

"You can take your ridiculous . . ."

"Please!" He silenced her with a kiss. "Consider us engaged."

"Make love to me."

"Not a chance!" That was putting it a little too strongly, of course.

"You've lost interest already?"

"Hardly." He found an especially pleasing place to rest his hand and was rewarded by her sensual squirming. "Let's talk about your book and that interesting scene I read."

She struggled until she was leaning over him. "I love you, Eric Sheffield."

"I thought you'd never admit it."

"Now you know." She cradled her head on his chest. "But why didn't you come here sooner? Or call?"

"I couldn't tell you how I felt over the phone, and I needed time to think."

"You were probably too busy with your store." She pretended to pout.

"I didn't want to come until my mind was wholly on you. Thanks to your personal appearance and some major management changes, we're going to salvage the

Loop store. Having you there with all your fans showed that the location still has potential. I think that calls for a celebration."

"What kind of celebration?"

"How about a honeymoon?"

"After our wedding?" She snuggled closer, inching the sheet down with her toes.

"I don't know if I can wait that long."

"Where should we go?"

"Here is nice."

"Not Paris, Vienna, Rome?"

"Later if you like, but I'm staying right here until you're ready to come home to Minneapolis with me. Is your book a problem?"

"I can finish it anywhere."

"Good."

"I have an uncle in the real estate business who can sell my house."

"Better."

"My sister has been trying to marry me off for years. She'll be glad to take care of everything if I let her be my matron of honor."

"Ah, back to wedding bells."

"Not bells, balloons."

"Balloons?"

"We can get married in my parents' garden. It's perfect for a small wedding. Your family, my family, a few dozen friends."

"Dozen?"

"Well, certainly under a hundred."

"That many?"

"We'll talk about it later."

"What about balloons?"

"I want bunches of balloons, hundreds and hundreds, red and pink and white, like the ones at the Romance Conference. After we're officially married, we'll cut all

188

the strings and watch them float away in a cobalt sky with big fluffy clouds shaped like unicorns and elves."

Her face was inches from his, almost demanding to be kissed. They turned at the same instant, facing each other side by side, motionless and blissful, generating a current that brought her into his arms with a throaty sigh.

They made delicious leisurely love. He filled her with rapture, slowly coaxing away the last remnant of her inhibitions, courting her with adoration, and taking her with deep, loving thrusts that lasted and lasted until she ravaged his mouth and welded his body to hers.

A moment came when her pleasure was so intense it became a new kind of pain and she cried out, not sure if she laughed or screamed. Moved beyond words, he loved her with his total being, holding back ocean currents and traveling to a new dimension for her. She was aware of everything: the warmth of his breath, the pulse in his throat, the rise and fall of his chest, the tension of his stomach, the flexing of his shoulders.

She could only endure the final convulsive rush of warmth because she knew there'd be another time and another and another. He whispered frenzied endearments that flowed through her like the undertow of a great wave. Her contractions became gentle flutters, and she clung to him, their limbs so entwined that all seemed to belong to both.

Bathing her with kisses and claiming her with words, he laughed aloud with happiness, holding her close until the drowsiness of undiluted joy washed over them.

"One other thing," she said euphorically, "you have to promise not to pop any of our wedding balloons."

"Why?" He curled a lock of black hair around his little finger.

"Someday I'll tell you." He was so beautiful she felt weepy.

"Tell me now."

"Absolutely not! I want our marriage to be like a good novel. Always a surprise on the next page."

"In a little while we'll turn another page. I have a plot twist you're going to remember for a long, long time."

LOOK FOR NEXT MONTH'S
CANDLELIGHT ECSTASY ROMANCES®:

All-new Candlelight Newsletter

An exceptional, *free* offer awaits readers of Dell's incomparable Candlelight Ecstasy and Supreme Romances.

Subscribe to our all-new CANDLELIGHT NEWSLETTER and you will receive—at absolutely no cost to you—exciting, exclusive information about today's finest romance novels and novelists. You'll be part of a select group to receive sneak previews of upcoming Candlelight Romances, well in advance of publication.

You'll also go behind the scenes to "meet" our Ecstasy and Supreme authors, learning firsthand where they get their ideas and how they made it to the top. News of author appearances and events will be detailed, as well. And contributions from the Candlelight editor will give you the inside scoop on how she makes her decisions about what to publish—and how *you* can try your hand at writing an Ecstasy or Supreme.

You'll find all this and more in Dell's CANDLELIGHT NEWSLETTER. And best of all, *it costs you nothing*. That's right! It's Dell's way of thanking our loyal Candlelight readers and of adding another dimension to your reading enjoyment.

Just fill out the coupon below, return it to us, and look forward to receiving the first of many CANDLELIGHT NEWSLETTERS—overflowing with the kind of excitement that only enhances our romances!

Dell **DELL READERS SERVICE—DEPT.** B393A
P.O. BOX 1000, PINE BROOK, N.J. 07058

Name_____

Address_____

City_____

State_____ Zip_____